Confessions of a D-List Supervillain

by

Jim Bernheimer

Dedication and Acknowledgements

For my family – Kim, Laura, and Marissa. You three keep me going no matter what. My brother Joe thanks for helping to inspire my creativity.

For my friends – Thank you for all the help you've given me along the way. Larry Hitt, thanks listening to all my crazy stories as a teenager. Dusty Gray, thanks for pretty much the same thing in the decades including and following my stint in the US Navy. Ted Vinzani, your assistance with editing and formatting is greatly appreciated. Same goes for Noel, Brian, Dave, Clell, Matthew Schocke and the novel critique group The Pendulum on the Permuted Press Message boards all deserve hearty thanks for their input along with Lindsey Schocke and Kathryn Ardell for the final edits. Fiona Hsieh, my cover artist, deserves plenty of credit for the artwork that enticed many of you to look at this book in the first place. I also want to thank David Wood at Gryphonwood Press for giving me my first break as a novelist.

For those I've lost – Jeff Dunlap and John Taladay. You were both great men taken from this earth too soon.

For the fans – you're few in number but growing steadily. Thank you for the encouragement.

Confessions of a D-List Supervillain was originally a novella in my collection *Horror, Humor, and Heroes*, Volume One.

Finally, one cannot write a story about a superhero or supervillain in a powered suit without acknowledging the influences of Marvel Comics for their creation of *Iron Man* and Robert Heinlein for his groundbreaking novel *Starship Troopers*.

Table of Contents

Confessions of a D-List Supervillain

Chapter One

I Went to New Orleans (and all I got was this lousy prisoner)

I'm so screwed.

They're coming for me and I'm no match for them.

There've been dozens of times I've wanted to quit the supervillain business, but never like right now! Hell, I was in semi-retirement when everything went to crap, delivering some orders to what few clients I still had.

This janitor's closet in a rundown warehouse is where I'll likely make my final stand. The alarms inside the armor warn me that power levels are down to twenty-two percent – not good. Below fifteen, the flight system won't activate.

I scan the walls looking for a power source, any electrical current that I can tap into. Nothing ... the building is as dead as I am about to be.

If this was just the Gulf Coast Guardians, I'd have a shot. Of the four Guardian teams, they're definitely the junior varsity squad. If it was the Biloxi Bugler, I'd kick his ass and mock him (and his sonic bugle) while I did it.

It's not. I'm not that lucky. I'm never that lucky. It's the story of my life. Instead, it's the Olympians, the foremost hero team in the whole world and I'm a minor supervillain at best.

Yeah, those Olympians, twelve college kids who disappeared on a cruise in the Mediterranean. A year later they returned with powers and training from the original Greek Gods. Against them, Calvin Matthew Stringel, reasonably talented, but hapless inventor currently known as "Mechani-CAL," doesn't stand a chance.

• • •

The power meter drops to twenty-one percent. Hermes is zipping through the main room, but if I stay still and conserve energy, maybe she'll give up.

Just because she is super fast doesn't mean she's super thorough! The lack of lighting in the building is hurting her and she's making lots of noise out there and being overly clumsy.

Of course, those *things* controlling her mind haven't quite mastered the operation of the fastest woman alive.

Yup, the world's been taken over and I missed it. All I know for certain is that The Evil Overlord was hiring geneticists like crazy late last year. Now these bugs, about twice the size of a grasshopper, are attached to everyone's neck and society seems to be reorganizing into a hive mentality. Granted, it would probably make standing in line more tolerable, but I'm not quite ready to sign up.

Given that it's been two weeks since this started and there has been no worldwide broadcast from the megalomaniac, it's a safe bet that this is an experiment gone awry rather than a plan masterfully executed. Good riddance to him anyway. The lousy cheapskate stopped using me as a supplier and stiffed me for two shipments of pulse cannons! Technically, I should thank him. Had he paid up, I probably wouldn't have wasted my time on that penny-ante jetpack sale in Montgomery and wouldn't have been in my suit when the bugs came.

The only reason I'm not already part of the "New World Order" is that I haven't taken off my battle armor since civilization was forcibly reorganized. Things are getting a bit ripe in the old Mark II CAL suit. I'd ventilate, but the stench would be a dead giveaway.

Laying low helped me up until yesterday, but it didn't last. It never does, does it? Initially, I only had to deal with the normal folks and was more than a match for plain old policemen and the National Guard. Puh-leaze! I might be a washed up, unemployable electrical engineer, called a "petty, second stringer, wannabe imitator" by Ultraweapon (with his fancy multimillion dollar suit), but I'm not a pushover. I've got force blasters, enhanced strength, and a flight pack.

Am I that much of a threat to the bugs? Maybe I'm all the threat that's left? God! That's a scary thought! Either way, the bugs trotted out the big guns. They didn't waste time sending other super groups after me. I get to tangle with the Olympians! It hasn't been much of a fight so far, unless getting my butt kicked from one end of New Orleans to the other is a "fight."

A jettisoned powerpack set to overload got me this far. Ares' dived on top of it to protect his teammates and possibly that thing on his neck. The blast didn't destroy his nigh-invulnerable body, probably just gave him a really irritating skin rash, but it did buy me enough time to fly a mile or so away before Apollo's fireball sent me crashing into this row of warehouses.

Wasting no time, I blew a hole into the next warehouse and the next one hoping it would look like I ran that way. Then, I found a hiding place here to assess the damage to my suit.

Hermes, a thin black woman who was a onetime NCAA champion track sprinter, continues to look around. She just won't leave. There's no choice. I have to try and take her.

Charge force blasters and set for wide area pulse dispersal. My neural interface issues the commands and I feel the suit respond. I'll waste power that I don't really have. She'll come at me like a missile with that metal rod of hers in her hand. Screw up and she'll give me the "Nancy Kerrigan treatment" a dozen times before I can blink.

It's not the first time someone's tried this stunt with her and there's no way it would work if she was "in control," but it's the best option I have. Bursting out of the closet, I get her attention. Sure enough, she accelerates. In the dimly lit warehouse, I trigger a flash from my waist mounted spotlight to partially blind her and immediately trigger the force pulse.

The embedded scanners still functioning register the gust of wind behind me as she stumbles out of control, smashing into empty crates. My auditory sensors pick up her moans, but they're fading as I sprint away. The rest will be hot on my heels. Normally, I'd be proud. I just took out an Olympian! How come I feel like I'm going to wet myself?

Screw it! Back out the way I came in! *Activate flight system!* I shoot right out the hole in the roof and directly into Apollo's fire bolt. *Fire retros! Fire retros!* They cushion the fall and I manage to land on the roof. Sixteen percent! Damn, that hurt! Don't just lie there waiting to die, move it!

Something smacks into the helmet and rings my bell. What now? Psionic blast, that means Aphrodite. There she is, leaping off her hover-sled. Sure, I've got her pinup, but I've never seen her up close before. Damn, she's hot! But she's not the most powerful, so maybe I can stop her. Shields almost down! Apollo's next fireball will start melting the suit with me in it. Suck it up Cal; you're not getting out of here alive. Might as well try to take one with me – maybe she'd even want me to?

Concentrated blast! Got her! Sorry, beautiful. Twelve percent! Maybe if I sprint to her hover-sled? Dodge left! Phew! That was close. Aw crap, she's getting back up; I didn't even do that right.

Apollo and Zeus both land between freedom and me. They're too strong to take in hand-to-hand combat, not that I'm going to get that close anyway.

I try another blast. Zeus shields it way too easily. Aphrodite stumbles to their side as Apollo conjures a big ass fireball. Funny, I didn't bring any marshmallows. All I have left is a tiny wiener and it's about to be roasted.

She speaks, "No! The colony wants him alive. You will join us in servitude. Zeus, overload his suit."

Now there's a change. Lame proclamations from the good guys. What's the world coming to?

Cerulean energy builds up around the Olympian. It's a pretty idiotic maneuver. I can absorb the energy and recharge. Even with the bugs, they can't be that stupid.

He falters, "Are you certain, Aphrodite?"

Her psi-bolt fires and stuns ... Apollo? Zeus spins toward her, but she nails him and he falls to the ground.

She looks at me and shouts, "Don't just stand there! Your blast was enough for me to overwhelm the damn thing on my neck. We've got to get out of here!"

Okay, new plan. Escape with the ultrahottie. Her idea's a helluva lot better than mine.

"I need some power!" I yell.

Stopping at Zeus, I grab his hand. Yeah, it is another technique copied from Ultraweapon, but who cares? What's "rich boy" going to do, sic more lawyers on me? Spread more lies about me stealing designs from him? Who cares? I drain the Thunder God for a quick recharge.

"Hurry up!" she exclaims.

Yeah, she sure is pretty ... pretty impatient that is. Twenty-six percent, twenty-nine percent, come on!

"I still need more."

She smacks the handlebars on her sled in frustration, "There's no time! The others will be coming."

The lady has a point. At full power, I wasn't exactly kicking butt and taking names. Thirty-three percent sounds like a winner.

Activate flight system! "How fast can those sleds go?"

She's already headed off the roof. "One-twenty!"

"Too slow! We can go faster if I carry you. Grab on!" Just about every guy's dream is to wrap their arms around Stacy Mitchell. She's the most heavily photographed woman in the world, and I never thought that it'd be happening to me. If I survive, it'll definitely go in my memoir, or at least in an e-mail submission to an adult magazine.

I scoop her off her seat and throttle up. Two hundred fifty miles per hour is my top speed unloaded, but I can easily hit two hundred with her. New Orleans is already fading into the background.

Over the rush of the wind she screams, "You're Mechanical, right?"

"It's actually Mechani-Cal. Oh, never mind. Just call me Cal."

"Whatever! Have you got a hideout or something we can use? Zeus might be down, but he's not out. He'll start tracking you eventually."

"Yeah, I've got a place near Pascagoula, but I want to head north for a minute or two more before we change directions, and then make for the Gulf of Mexico."

"Do you know anyone else that isn't infected?" She sounds almost hopeful.

"I was looking for that shelter the Swamp Lord was broadcasting about on the shortwave. It's supposed to be around here. Do you want to try for it instead?"

My external sensors strain to pick up, "Don't bother. We were just there."

"I guess that makes my answer 'No.' I'm making the direction change now. We'll head out about a mile or so into the Gulf and then slow down and fly just above the waves, below radar. Poseidon wasn't with you was he?"

There's a bit of fear in her voice. "No, he's looking for submarines in the Atlantic. Over the water's fine, but don't go too slow. Another bug could land on me."

• • •

Forty minutes later, I'm on the ground at my "lair." It's a small junkyard whose owners sold off after Hurricane Katrina. I picked it up for next to nothing, which was pretty much what I had at the time. Still, there's lots of scrap metal and wiring to use. And like anything else, a villain's hideout is about three things, location, location, and location. In this case, the more remote the location is the better.

"Are you okay, Aphrodite? Should I call you Stacy?"

"Yeah, I'm just a little nasty from the sea spray. Let's just stick to Aphrodite for now, okay?" She surveys my property for a moment, before adopting a sad look on her face. "Please tell me this is just a place to stop and not your hideout? Do you have a shower, or should I just look for the outhouse?"

Great, the girl of everyone's dreams just dissed my hideout. I sputter, "Wait, I've got more underground! It gets better, trust me!"

Is it just my imagination, or did I sound a little like a junior high schooler there? I make a mental note not to ask her to sign the swimsuit calendar hanging above the workbench.

Her demeanor doesn't improve once she gets inside. "Weren't expecting company, were you?"

Moving some clutter out of the way, I reply. "No, but up here is *meant* to look like a junkyard." I pull the lever in the pantry to reveal the secret staircase and cut on the lights.

She gets to the bottom of the steps and looks around, "And this is supposed to be better?"

Come to think of it, the downstairs is a bit messy too. But damn she's bitchy! So much for all those fantasies. "Bathroom and shower are over there. Clean towels are on the shelves. I'll check the shortwave. We're off the Internet here. I'm pretty sure the bugs have people looking for any IP traffic. Are you okay?"

She's shaking and looks like she's going to be sick. "I just need to clean up, excuse me." She runs into the bathroom and slams the door so hard that it comes off the upper hinge, leaving me standing in the middle of the room.

Quickly, I activate the passive sensors placed throughout the junkyard and swap in a series of fresh powercells for the nearly exhausted ones in my suit. The old ones go on the charging unit and the amplifiers in my helmet pick up the retching of the "Luv Goddess" into the toilet. I should cut her a bit of slack, coming off of being mind controlled, and try to be a better host. I'm running a hand scanner over the exterior of the armor, performing some diagnostics when the shower starts. It's tempting to cut on the camera in the bathroom – to make certain she's okay – naturally.

I'm a criminal, a thief, and an arms dealer. I'm not a Peeping Tom. Then again, there's just one little command line between me and the pinup heroine, and she's "nekkid!"

Fortunately, I'm blessed with a very flexible set of morals – almost professional gymnast flexible. I put a gauntlet on the pad to transfer the command when her voice interrupts me, "Cal?"

"Yes."

Her tone is much less angry, "Listen, I'm sorry if I didn't sound thankful for you helping me out. I'm pretty weak right now and I need to charge my powers."

Well there's a nice change. "Hey no problem! Take as much time as you need."

There's a bit of laughter. "You don't understand, Cal. You know all those rumors that my powers are sexual in nature?"

My heart beats faster. Could it be? "Uh, yeah I'd heard a few. Aren't you always denying it?"

"It's not something I'll admit in public, but the rumors are true. I could do this by myself, but trust me, it'll go much faster if you get out of your suit and join me."

No friggin way! "Sure! Just give me a minute or two to get out of my armor!"

The absolute hottest woman on the planet is in my shower and waiting for me to come in there and charge her powers! Thank you, Lord! This makes up for all the times I've been screwed over. This makes up for the two years behind bars after the Bugler beat me as "ManaCALes," before I made the armor. This makes up for every break I never got. This makes up for ... Oh hell, this needs to be recorded for posterity. *Activate internal cameras. Record lower-level bathroom.* This is going to be great! This is going to be fantastic!

This is ... a trap? No! No! No! She's not even naked and she has her wrist communicator activated! I glance at the external display. Nothing, but then again, the Olympians could probably be all over the place. Shit! What am I going to do?

"What's taking you so long?" I see her whispering into her communicator. We now return to our regularly scheduled episode of *Cal Can't Catch a Break!*

"Sorry, it's going to take about five minutes to get out of the armor." Okay, bolt-box time! Spare powercells go in as well as two cases of NASA food paste, some goodies I picked up at a gadget swap meet, the laptop, and the half-finished MARK III CAL suit that I've been working on for the past two years. There's no way they're getting that!

"Cal, will you hurry up! I'm getting lonely in here."

"Almost done!" Smacking the big red "panic" button on the wall, I activate the not-so-passive defenses. Gun emplacements mounted in rusted hulks come to life with active targeting scanners. Big surprise! There are several heat signatures out there. My "junkyard doggie" bursts out of a dilapidated doublewide trailer. He's a big old loveable hunk of iron with claws for hands and four pulse cannons mounted on him.

If I'm lucky, he'll last two minutes.

The sirens alert the lovely in the bathroom that all is not well with her little plan. She bursts out! "You could have gone the easy way, but no! I get my bug back when I bring you in!"

"No thanks. I think I'll pass."

"Fine you third-rate Ultrawannabe. I won't be gentle!"

Psi-bolts smash into my shields, letting me know that the earlier ones were just love taps. She's got a thick skin, so I give her a full broadside. Aphrodite leaps out of the way, but trips over all the technojunk strewn about. I've got to finish her fast! Shields continue to hold against her barrage. I fire again, slightly to her left driving her toward a beat up freezer and fire right at it when she's in front.

My target dodges, but the secondary explosion from all the chemicals stored in the fridge catches her. I seal the suit against the fumes and activate the two-minute self-destruct. Picking up her communicator, I scream into it, "You'll never take me alive, Olympians!"

Dropping it, I crush it under my feet and look at the stunned Aphrodite. I could leave her and let the destruct finish her, but it's obvious she's still under their control. The effect has to wear off! I give her a heavy Taser pulse to make sure she's out, throw her over my shoulder, and I grab the bolt-box.

One glance at a still functioning screen shows that the doggy's getting pounded. I liked this base. Oh well, two miles of tunnel to fly through and then north to the backup base, "The Pig Sty."

• • •

"Where am I?"

"My other base." No need to tell her that she's in South Eastern Alabama at an old pig farm near the Mobile River.

"Let me go!" A psi-bolt slams into the reinforced steel door of the cell area. The previous owner of this base used barbed wire of all things for a cell – idiot! Fortunately, I spent some time fixing it up. Still, I already miss the junkyard.

"No!" I shout.

"I can contact them telepathically."

"Not from sixty feet below ground in a shielded cell you can't."

Five more psi-bolts impact against the door. The last one is noticeably weaker. "Please, Cal, I need to go! I won't tell them you're still alive. Just let me go."

"Why do you want to go so badly?"

She turns on the water works and I flip on the shielded box camera that I installed behind her polished metal "mirror" an hour ago.

Aphrodite is on the floor crying and convulsing. Rerouting the camera feed over to the suit, I walk to the cell. Scooping a head off some robot thing I never finished building; I pull back the metal plate and stick the robot head up to the peephole.

"Are you okay in there?" *Wham!* The head is blasted out of my hand by a rather strong burst of energy from her. The heads-up-display shows her with a wild look in her eyes as she leaps to her feet. I barely get the cover back on before her fists and mental energy begin impacting on the door. She was playing at being weak and tried for a sucker punch.

"That wasn't very nice! I'm trying to save you."

"I don't want to be saved! Let me out! I'll kill you! I'll kill you! Let me out!"

"That really wasn't a bright move. Suppose you had killed me just there? You'd starve in there in a few days."

Instead of a proper response all I get is screams and her pounding on the door. Arguing with the mentally unstable isn't very productive. I make a few more attempts to communicate and decide to let her work out some of her excess energy.

Meanwhile, I need to figure out what the hell I'm going to do.

• • •

In the morning, I open the suit's service panel, dump the "poop chute," change the water bottle, and screw in the food paste packet for breakfast. It's a fairly self-contained existence, and since I'm not very choosy, I can keep it up for at least six months. If it's good enough for the astronauts up in the space station, it is good enough for me. There's a horrible thought, what are those poor SOB's up there thinking right now, or did the bugs send a space-capable superhuman up there already?

Stacy Mitchell, on the other hand, probably doesn't care for steak and eggs in an oversized toothpaste tube. The freezer is full of TV dinners and frozen waffles. I make her a tray and switch over to the containment cell feed.

"Shit! When did she do that?" I look at the display in dismay. She blew up the sink and toilet! There's water everywhere! I interface with the main computer and tell it to cut off the water to that side of the base. She didn't destroy the bunk – that's where she's curled up at the moment.

Sliding the top bar back, I look in, not wanting to tip my hand about the surveillance camera. "Hey! What happened to your sink and toilet?"

"Go to hell!"

"Well, I don't see how this is making *my* life more difficult. The water will drain when I open the valve and I can probably replace the toilet and sink, but I'm not going to if you're just going to destroy them again."

"I'm going to kill you!" she says slowly, full of murderous intent. On the plus side, she sounds more coherent and less foaming-at-the-mouth today.

"I thought you were the 'good' guys? I guess that doesn't mean as much anymore."

"It's going to be slow. I'll make you beg before I kill you unless you let me go right now!"

It's actually somewhat humorous listening to her. "Would you like some breakfast? Can't kill me on an empty stomach, you know."

Her energy goes through the tiny opening and hits the wall.

"So, not very hungry today? Okay then, I'll bring you a bucket and send it in through an access door."

"I'm not cleaning this up, you bastard."

"You don't need to. I told you the water will drain. The bucket is in case you need to go to the bathroom."

"What?"

"Well I'm guessing you're going to need to go to the bathroom sooner or later, and your toilet isn't getting fixed anytime soon, princess. Before you get any cute ideas, I can filter my air. If you start flinging crap around your cell like some kind of goddamn monkey, you're the only one that's going to smell it. I've got a second cell down here and if you can be good for a few days we'll move you to it."

Her feet splash across the room as I shut the metal plate. She bangs on the door. "You can't keep me in here like some kind of animal! I need a bug! Get me a bug!"

"Why?"

"I need one!" Her fists start pounding against the door.

"Again, why? They've turned you into some kind of slave. You should be happy to be free of them."

"Please, just get me a bug. I'll do anything you want. It hurts."

That little exchange gave me volumes of information. However these bugs were made, whatever was in them is highly addictive. Explains why nobody just squished the bugs and went on their merry way.

"How do the bugs make you feel?"

She's sobbing now, but still hammering away at the door. "They make you feel incredible. It must be like what people feel if I use my powers on them, except it's so much more! Just get me one. Stun me and dump me somewhere, I don't care. I won't tell them where you are. I don't even know where we are!"

I try to sound as calm as possible. "Stacy, I can't do that. Everyone thinks we're dead. I intend to keep it that way and you need to try to get out from under their influence."

"Don't call me Stacy! I'm Aphrodite!"

"No. Aphrodite's a hero, an Olympian. You're a woman named Stacy with an addiction. Aphrodite would know that these things were made by The Evil Overlord to enslave humanity."

"I don't care about him. I don't care about you. Just let me go."

The argument goes on for awhile, but I tire of listening and walk away. I've met a few addicts in my lifetime. Turning on some music, I head up to the workshop. Eventually, I'll have to go out again and the Olympians are still out there. My chances will be better if I finally finish the MARK III CAL suit.

• • •

"Tell me about yourself, Cal?"

Two days have passed. Stacy is trying new tactics with me. Instead of screaming and threats, (which got progressively more graphic) she wants to be my friend. It won't last, but I've got to hope she can kick this thing. She doesn't know the "lament of the nerd." Every geek that gets into their late twenties looks back at all the girls/women that crossed his path and sees how the good-looking ones were always trying to get something. How many of them had I helped in study groups? They never overlooked the bad acne and eczema that followed me to UCLA. How many tires did I change and computers did I fix, hoping for a number from a grateful coed? How many boxes and pieces of furniture did I carry because a pretty pair of lips asked me?

At some point every schmuck like me takes stock of his life and faces the reality that the really good-looking ones, and even most of the average ones, are just going to try and use them.

"UCLA, Electrical Engineering major. I played drums in a cover band. I like music. Don't really care for long walks on the beach. Graduated top of the class and was hired straight out by Promethia." The voice modulator in the suit disguises my hatred for the name of Ultraweapon's company.

"I saw it in your file that you stole a bunch of designs from Lazarus, so you could become a cheap knock-off."

Oh, she found a big sore spot with me. "I did not! That was his lawyers and their smear campaign."

"That's not what I read. So, you're a little worker bee with delusions of adequacy, stealing from a genius like Lazarus Patterson." She's shifting tactics again, baiting me, and like an idiot I'm falling for it.

"Genius! Hah! Patterson might have created synth-muscle, but that's about it. Everything else in his Ultraweapon suit was designed by engineers just like me on his R&D staff. *I* made his original force blasters! *Me!*"

"...and you stole the designs and went into a life of crime."

"No! I quit Promethia when they refused to put my name on the patents and acknowledge my work. I went to work at Ubertex, but then Promethia's lawyers showed up with their three-year no compete clause in my employment contract, and Ubertex cut me loose."

"Oh, you poor baby." There's no sympathy in her voice.

"Bitch! After that, Promethia spread the word about my 'poor performance' and basically black-balled me from pretty much every high tech job on both coasts. I came up with a small power compressor, and when I tried to file patent on it, guess what? Promethia dragged me into court and said it was derivative from items they were working on, and the court took my invention and gave it to them."

She's openly laughing now. "You must have been heartbroken!"

"If you're trying to get me to come in there, it's not happening. Just finish your TV dinner and put it on the cart. I'm leaving. Goodnight, Stacy."

"You're pathetic, Stringel. Go ahead and hide down in this hole, you rat. The moment you surface, the bugs will get you. Maybe I'll let you experience them and then take your bug away, just to watch you suffer."

A quick jerk of the head shuts off the external microphones. I ran right into her trap. If she had held off, I'd have probably told her about the humiliating string of jobs in the months afterwards, or Promethia actually coming after me to garnish my wages. I finally did snap and built a crude version of *my* force blasters and took the name ManaCALes. After knocking over a few jewelry stores, I tried a bank or two in Biloxi. That's when I got caught by the Bugler.

A guy with a sonic bugle beat me! The lamest jackass to ever put on a cape kicked my tail. It was a bad omen to start my career as a supervillain. I served twenty-six months of a five-year sentence in prison, but the time in the joint was actually pretty productive. I made contacts among the bad guys that passed through the maximum security prison for "supers." All that free time not trying to keep some stupid job and paying rent allowed me to design the MARK I suit.

After being released, I didn't even bother trying to reenter society. In addition to all of Promethia's slurs, I now had the label of convicted felon on my resume. That wouldn't look promising to most potential employers.

That is, of course, unless those new employers were also convicted felons. Diabolical masterminds just can't go through the Internet and arm their minions. I entered the highly competitive world of arms manufacturing for enterprising criminals. It's true that much of my MARK I suit was built off of Ultraweapon's designs, but I didn't do the stealing. I bartered them off of one of his enemies and she traded them for four cases of first-generation pulse pistols.

As I look at the MARK III lying on the bench and begin attaching synth-muscle to the actuators, I recall the good old days. Money was coming in. The MARK I was complete and I even got some revenge on the Bugler. That's when I started working with Vicky.

Contrary to Stacy's assertions, I'm not a "nose picking, never gonna get laid" virgin. Vicky was a buyer for The Evil Overlord, procuring weaponry from independent contractors such as myself. She liked my work and she actually liked me. I became a preferred supplier to the Overlord's armory and even started building the MARK II suit I'm wearing right now.

With the left leg actuator finished, I take a break and bring up my favorite first-person-shooter on the main screen, after checking to make sure the bitch downstairs is still confined. I miss Vicky. After committing my first robbery in the MARK II, I called her. She was going to fly out for a celebration and take my presentation for building moderately low-cost powersuits to the Overlord himself. I would have had a backlog of work that would make me filthy stinking rich and Vicky was going to resign after she got the deal approved. It was the perfect plan. There was just one small problem standing in the way of that happily ever after.

Vicky was in the Overlord's Omega Base when he triggered the self-destruct, trying to destroy the Olympians and the West Coast Guardians. They all escaped, naturally. She didn't.

The new buyer was this sleazy suit named Paul. Paul also liked my work. In fact, he liked it so much that he had some of the Overlord's in-house guys take the pulse cannons apart and reverse engineer the design to manufacture them without any markup.

That's Darwinism in the villain food chain. There really wasn't much I could do about it either. Even the bad guys were finding ways to screw me. That forced me to resume the other side of the business, while trying to land the next big contract. I went back to being a goon for hire.

General Devious recruited me into her Heroes Outmatched by Rampaging Destructive Executioner Squads. Yeah, I was a member of that idiotic HORDES group. The idea of over a hundred villains trying to work together didn't pan out as well as everyone thought.

Against all four Guardians groups, the Olympians, and countless other solo heroes, things went from bad to worse. It's the only time I ever actually fought against Ultraweapon. There's not even really a long story to what happened. That fight consisted of less than a minute of me getting my ass thoroughly kicked. It took three months to get the suit right after retreating as fast as I could – at less than half-speed.

Whoever upgraded those force blasters on his suit did a helluva job. I started on the MARK III that night, worked feverishly for two weeks, and then quit. I woke up and smelled the coffee. The bitter truth was I didn't have the brainpower or the budget to compete with Promethia's Research and Development department. There was no way I would ever be able to beat Ultraweapon.

So, I went into semi-retirement, pulling the occasional job just to fill the coffers. I did custom orders for the lower-level criminals and tried my best to stay away from the larger crime organizations, and more importantly the upper echelon of heroes. Chickenshit? Yes, but it kept me out of prison while I struggled to make a living.

Chapter Two

Songs That Get Stuck in Your Head

As the first week with my prisoner comes to a close, I'm seriously contemplating fulfilling her request, stunning and dumping her somewhere, like she wants. Becoming a true hermit is sounding more appealing by the hour.

I trigger the external sound feed and hear her screaming, "Will you shut that damn song off!"

"Oh, did I leave that song looping for the last six hours? I'm sorry."

"At least play something that isn't shit!"

"Biz would be offended. I love this song. In fact, guess what's on tap for the next six hours?"

Biz Markie's *Just A Friend*, it's a guilty pleasure song if ever there was one. I'm not bragging, but I do a mean karaoke version of it. Surprisingly, Stacy stopped her usual death threats and went into great detail about how much she hated this particular song.

Naturally, I've been, giving her "Da Biz" ever since. Part of me is trying to get her to focus on something other than trying to get another bug attached to her neck. Then there's the other part, the one that's had to put up with her crap and is sick and tired of it. Okay, I'm a spiteful little man. I accept that I have issues. That's not the point. Ms. Mitchell is damn lucky that I don't have homicidal tendencies.

"Are you going to use the knockout gas again tonight?" she hisses as the song starts up again. *Was that a plea?*

Maybe I'll switch it out with the live version I've got around here somewhere. Either way, I'm lying. I'm actually drugging her food and waiting a bit before releasing some compressed air. What bad guy has tanks of chloroform hanging around at their "backup" base? Even if I had that kind of money, I'm nowhere near that anal, but I'm beginning to wish I was.

"Look, I gotta sleep too, princess. There's that old cliché about the bad guy falling asleep and the hero escaping. Happens way too often in my line of work, so forgive me for taking a few precautions, okay?"

"I'll bet! You're probably in here indulging in some sick fantasy time, you prick! I know your type. I saw them enough even before I got my powers."

"Newsflash, you were hot, but now you're not even lukewarm. Go and look at yourself in the mirror. You haven't showered in three days, you've only changed your clothes once, and the toothbrush is still in its plastic case. There was a time when I thought you were the hottest thing on the planet. Right now the only thing you could attract is some flies! Have some damn pride, woman! I'm hoping you hit rock bottom before you start growing fungus."

Stacy starts screaming and goes quickly from raging to damn near incoherent. I go back to calibrating the new headgear on the Mark III armor. I've hit a minor snag in all of this. I'm running out of synth-muscle. Of course, there was plenty back at my main base. Or at least there used to be. All that's left now is a big, smoking crater.

I walk over to a storage closet with a feeling of nostalgia. Inside is the old Mark I. It looks so flimsy and primitive now. That beat-up old black suit doesn't have enough of Promethia's chief invention in it either, but the suit I'm wearing does.

What if Stacy escapes and I'm in the Mark I? It's going to take a good three days to strip all the components out of the II and work it into the new one. Even in her condition, could I take her in the old Mark I?

Hanging next to the suit is an item that evokes a scoffing laugh from me. It's quite possibly my most ridiculous invention ever. The previous owner of this hideout was a client of mine – Hillbilly Bobby, a country bumpkin with more strength than common sense. He paid me to make him several power clubs – force field generators strapped to two-by-fours. I'll admit, they weren't exactly my crowning achievements, but I was pretty short on cash at the time, like always.

Not surprisingly, Bobby ended up in prison. I think it was The Bugler or Andydroid who brought him in. I shake my head and pull out the old Mark I. I'll spend the rest of the day trying to tune it up and switch into it tonight.

• • •

"Wake up, princess. Don't go back to sleep on me. What would you like for breakfast this morning? I have waffles and . . . waffles – your choice."

Stacy is sprawled face-down on the floor next to her cot. She was her usual ranting lunatic self five minutes ago. I struggle with the interface mounted on the outside of the door. This old suit doesn't quite match up with the controls. It's just another insult added to injury. I'm also roughly fifteen pounds heavier than when I last wore the Mark I. It's just like pulling out a pair of pants that hasn't been worn in years and expecting it to fit. I feel like a cybernetic sausage.

"C'mon, get up. Let's see that beautiful face."

After issuing the command three times, I send the breakfast cart in through the access hatch. She's still not responding. This is what I was afraid of. Do I go in there and see if she's okay, or do I just stay and watch for awhile to see if she's playing possum?

Climbing back up the staircase, I get to the main console and bring up the surveillance camera. I skim through the last few minutes. She was awake, screaming and pacing. Stacy starts shaking and then stumbles. She looks like she's having some kind of a seizure. *Charge force blasters.* Crap, I forgot. This suit doesn't have the advanced cerebral interface. I whisper, "Charge force blasters."

I'm running this time; once again it takes me a few tries to interface with the cellblock controller to get the main door open. I finally get in there and approach her. The smell of vomit and urine forces me to activate my filters and I roll her over.

Unless she can fake blue lips, she's in real trouble. Even in my other base, I didn't really have a clinic. I do have a first aid kit mounted on the wall in the hallway. That's about it.

The next few minutes pass in a blur. I manage to get her swollen tongue out of her mouth and "bag" her to get her breathing. The needle on the adrenaline shot breaks on her thick skin and I resort to doing chest compressions with my powersuit to get her heart beating. It takes a few minutes before I can detect a steady pulse. I strap her to a gurney. Stacy might not be able to get out of the restraints in her condition, but I've got to be sure. Rigging up a crude monitor, I gather the dirty sheets and leave her cell.

"If this is what freeing everyone else is going to be like, I shouldn't even bother." She doesn't answer.

Thirty minutes later, the monitors alert me. Stacy's coming around. I stop what I'm doing and head back down into the cellblock.

Through the cameras, I watch her struggle against the bindings. She collapses after two minutes. Opening the door, I step in hesitantly with my blasters charged and my shield strength at this suit's peak. A pair of pitiful psi-bolts hit me. They barely register on my defenses.

"Calm down."

"What happened?" she asks blearily.

"You had a seizure. I think you're okay, now."

Her response is a raspy cough mixed with halting words. "I'm not okay. I'm never going to be okay, again. Either let me go or go ahead and let me die."

I ignore her and grab a sports bottle. "You don't mean that. Here, drink some water."

She resists feebly, but I get the straw into her mouth. "I mean it. Give me back to the bugs or just kill me."

"You were given powers by a bunch of ancient gods. Do you think they want you to give up? Didn't you swear some kind of oath to them?"

"They don't matter anymore. Nothing does."

My career as a motivational speaker isn't going anywhere. It's a safe bet that she's either at rock bottom or she's hit and started digging. "C'mon Stacy, work with me here. It's already been a week. Whatever these things make, it's got to be almost out of your system. Just give me another week. If you still want to leave then, I'll stun you and dump you somewhere."

When did I develop a blind spot for damsels in distress? Damn it!

"Do you promise?"

"Sure. I'll even promise to stop playing that song. Just make it another seven days and if you want to leave, I'll let you."

She breathes a huge sigh, before resorting to a threat. "You better not be lying."

I bring over the breakfast cart and start feeding her. "Just get your strength back. You won't be any use to your masters like this."

After finishing one waffle and a few spoonfuls of dried banana chips covered in syrup, she shakes her head and can't eat anymore. She stares at me for a second, "Why are you in that prehistoric relic?"

"I'm upgrading the other suit, for the next time I have to fight."

Stacy laughs, a sad, bitter sound and says, "You still think you have a chance. We were sent out to collect any people with creative talent. Honestly, you were pretty far down that list. What are you going to do? Upgrade your stealth suite? Increase the power output of your blasters?

No matter how hard you try, you're not going to out-create the rest of the world. You should just give up."

I stare at her. She can't see my jaw hanging open in disbelief. "Are you able to read my mind through this helmet?"

"No, I just know you brainy types. It's exactly what Lazarus does every time someone manages to beat him. He'd ignore me for days on end, huddle with his staff, and they'd brainstorm how to make the suit better. I'm just telling it like it is. If you could have made a better suit before, you would have. Do whatever you want, but I can tell you that you aren't going to win."

Her eyes don't have that malicious gleam like during her earlier taunts. There's just resignation. I storm out of the room, knowing she's right. Sealing the door, I stand in the hallway, uncertain of what to do next. The only real difference between me and Stacy is that my cell is bigger than hers.

• • •

Afternoon finds her in better spirits. Stacy seems to be getting her appetite back. I release her from the gurney and she doesn't try to attack me. When she asks for a fresh set of clothes and heads behind the partition to take a shower, I get my hopes up.

She looks like she's improved, so I ask, "Are you feeling better?"

"Yeah, I can deal."

Inside my suit, I smile. Stacy is turning a corner. "I'm glad to hear that."

"Well, it's only a week. I can get through it. I've made it this far."

The grin fades. She's delusional. I have a super nut job on my hands. Searching the main computer, I look around for anything dealing with addicts. Not surprisingly, the pickings are slim. I have lots of bootleg software, plans for all kinds of stolen technology, thousands of illegal movies and music files, but my self-improvement section is pretty . . . lame.

Yeah, I've known a few addicts in my life, but I didn't say that I cured any. Generally, I'd say, "Hey, you've got some serious problems. You should get some help." I fix gadgets, not people.

Lacking any other resources, I go with my gut instinct. I set the clock in her cell to count only three seconds for every four. Her days just got six hours longer. I might not be able to out-create the entire world, but cheating can narrow the gap.

I try to take advantage of her suddenly good nature. "Anything you're willing to tell me about the world outside would be nice. What are the bugs making everyone do?"

"They're organizing themselves into work-groups and building factories."

"What are they making in the factories?"

"I don't think they're making anything yet."

"Yeah, that sounds like the Overlord's Modus Operandi. Draft an endless supply of labor and put them to work. All the creative people are probably slaving away designing things. The only problem is that there is no one to give the orders to start production. That's the problem with megalomaniacs, what do they do when they enslave the world? They want more and better weapons. Who would they use them against?" I snap my fingers. "Hey, I just thought of something, how do those bugs get through your skin? You Olympians aren't exactly fragile."

"It's absorbed through the skin, I think."

"What about Andydroid, the Cyber Dudes, and the Silicon Sisterhood?"

She pauses for a moment before answering, a hint of guilt in her voice, "They were captured and deactivated, or ...."

I finish it for her, "... or they got the Humpty Dumpty treatment, but somehow you can justify this."

"It's ... regrettable."

Biting my tongue, I cut the intercom off. Regrettable is a word for it, alright. I don't know why I'm letting this get to me. It's not like I'm a big fan of any of those clowns. Hearing her casually say that sends a jolt of disappointment through me. Maybe I'd expected more from her. I stare uselessly at the pair of powersuits on my work tables. I'm not in a league with people like Lazarus Patterson. Compared to him, I'm a rube, like Hillbilly Bobby.

Wait just a damn second! That might be it.

• • •

Stacy was right. I can't out think all of them. All of my designs have gotten progressively more complicated as I looked for ways to improve and add new features. But this suit won't be used for crimes. That means no stealth suites, countermeasures, or niceties like cargo space. It has only one purpose – to fight.

I remove the force blaster from the right arm. The left will be my sole built-in weapon and the extra space allows me to install more synth-muscle. Next I get a pulse cannon and add a rifle grip. My main weapon will be external and powered independently from my suit. The force field generator from Bobby's useless wooden club gets attached to a fifteen pound sledgehammer. The simplicity of the design is what makes it so beautiful. The Mark III is going to be a crude tank, and I like it!

The good news is tempered with the bad. Stacy is still counting down the hours until I let her go. There are regular withdrawal symptoms and she still degenerates into a foaming at the mouth lunatic at least three times during her thirty hour "day."

After the latest bout I opted to give her "Da Biz."

As the song ends, she screams, "You miserable lying bastard!"

"Beg pardon?"

"I know exactly how long that blasted song is. You messed with the damn clock. You're not going to let me go!"

Shit! It's yet another instance of me missing the obvious. So much for our somewhat amicable relationship. "Well, I am a criminal. Lying isn't exactly beneath me."

Her psi-bolts smash into the cell door and wall. She's really pissed and I'm kicking myself in the ass for insisting Stacy try to regain her strength. I divert auxiliary power to the fields around the cell block and struggle getting the Mark I's gauntlets back on.

"Don't make me hurt you Stacy," I warn.

"In that tin can you're wearing? I'd like to see you try."

A command cuts off her lights and plunges the cell into darkness. If she can't see, her blasts will be less concentrated. I slip around to the backside access panel and interface with the main computer. I fire up some of the loudest stuff in my audio library and turn the lights back on at maximum brightness and fire off some Taser pulses. Her instincts are good and she dodges the first two. On the third one, I use the access panel where I send her food tray in. She didn't suspect that.

With her physiology, she won't be out long, ten minutes at the most. I run back upstairs and grab the gutted Mark II helmet. I make a few hurried adjustments to it and go back and stun her again.

Later, she comes to. "What the hell is this?"

"It's the hottie in the iron mask. Sorry about the haircut. You'd be even more upset if you could see it. Food tube is the one on the left. Water tube is the one on the right."

"I'll rip it off."

"Probably not. It's on you pretty tight – you don't have the leverage. Wouldn't try your psi-bolts either, they're liable to rebound. That'd hurt."

"I hate you!"

Over her rant, I mock her. "You'll thank me later. I'm just trying to get you cleaned out. Be glad that you still have the free will to hate. If you had one of those things on you, you wouldn't give a rat's ass about hating me. I'm going to cut you off in a second. I'll check back with you in a bit, but I've got work to do. I do believe that this 'third-rate Ultrawannabe' took you out in my 'ancient relic' of a powersuit. Know something? This calls for some celebratory music. Do you like Biz Markie?"

• • •

Things have been quiet for the last five days. She hasn't said a word to me. I keep telling her what's going on, but I'm guessing that Stacy's probably a little bitter. My time is consumed in the workshop on the Mark III. I've been obsessing over it and the project is really coming together.

Over the intercom, I say, "It's almost done. I'm putting on the finishing touches now."

She looks in the direction of the speakers and surprisingly, utters her first words, "Whoopee flipping do."

I cut the music off and say, "Do try and contain your excitement."

"It's not going to matter, Cal. You're just too stupid to realize that."

"So Stacy, to what do I owe this honor? Still want to leave and go get your fix?"

"If I said 'no,' would you believe me?"

"Probably not."

"Then I won't bother lying. I'm sure your new suit is just spiffy, congratulations," she deadpans.

"I think I liked you better when you were quiet."

"Set me free and you won't have to listen to me. You've got your brand new suit. Everyone will be quaking in fear. So, what happens to me when you go out in your new suit and they still beat you?"

"You might have given up, but I haven't. Someone out there can beat this even if you're too weak to try. Maybe there's a resistance out there somewhere. If so, they might need me."

"If that's the lie you want to tell yourself, Cal, by all means, cling to it. I can tell you that anyone worth a damn was captured a long time ago. Wanna hear how it went down? Most of them came running to our Headquarters, because we said we weren't infected and we sent out notifications to everyone useful. Your invite must have gotten lost in the mail. Heroes kept coming and we were waiting for them."

I stop midway through dressing in the new suit as she goes into lengthy detail about the subjugation of the planet's heroes. It's sickening. I button the suit up and start the power up sequence. Grabbing the power hammer and pulse rifle, I storm down into the block area.

I check her cell feed and open the door. "How about I take that helmet off of you and give you a chance to fight your way out."

She isn't terribly impressed. "Bring it on, *Calvin*. This is your masterpiece? This? You've got to be kidding me."

Before I know it, I'm triggering the unlatching mechanism on her helmet. It falls to the ground with a clatter and once again, I'm staring at her. Even with a horrible haircut and days of not being able to wash her face, she's gorgeous. Her psi-bolts hit my shields and knock me around a little bit. A blast from my pulse rifle narrowly misses, but in such a confined space it batters her into the wall. Stacy staggers back to her feet. I absorb her next four blasts, and my pulse rifle blows her into the adjacent cell. She's bruised and battered, barely able to stand.

Dropping the rifle, I grab Stacy with both hands as she tries to flee out the opening into the passageway. Somewhere in all this, she became a symbol of all my failures and all the people who've beaten me. It's wrong. I know it, but can't stop myself.

I push her against the wall face-first and hold her there for a minute, unsure of what to do next.

"Just finish me," I pick up from my external microphones. "What the hell are you waiting for?"

It's a good question.

Do I have anything left to prove?

The answer is no, at least not to myself. I look back at the cell block. Both are ruined, I either have to kill her or let her go. I won the battle, but lost the war.

She struggles in vain. I keep her face turned away. Her psi-bolts can't get to me. Time passes and Stacy stops, waiting for me to reach a decision.

I set her down on the ground and keep her from falling. "Can you stand?"

"What are you doing?"

"Setting you free. Time to go rejoin your masters. This is pointless."

Stacy clearly doesn't understand. "What?"

"Go up the steps, through the main control room. There's another set of steps and the elevator is on the far wall. The exit key code is 8675309 – Tommy Tutone's song. You'll have to climb sixty feet up a ladder after that, but you'll be on the surface. I'm sure you'll have a bug on you within the hour if you get a move on."

She immediately starts in that direction, but pauses on the steps. "What about you?"

"I'll set the self-destruct."

"In that case, you should just stun me and use this time to grab whatever you're going to take with you to your next base. I won't be able to keep anything from them."

"There's no next base. I'm not leaving."

Either her injuries are worse than I thought, or my words get the better of her.

She shakes her head in disbelief. "They aren't going to buy it. You have another base. There's always another base! They won't believe you faked your death twice."

"No faking this time."

"You're just giving up?"

"Why not? You did. Look, you've been here seventeen days, Stacy. You used to be one of the most powerful heroes on the planet and you can't beat this. If you couldn't, then no one else is going to be able to. I can't save the human race. I'm tired of all this."

Her confusion draws a sigh and I continue, "You said it yourself, Stacy. The bugs have a limited set of orders. They start with capturing everyone, building factories, and designing weapons. When people start dying, are they going to make babies for replacement workers, or is the human race going to die off?"

She stammers, "I don't ... I don't know."

"My guess is no – they don't have that programming. And going up there means I'll end up in a big old fight with any available heroes and villains they send my way. This armor should let me beat the first few, but eventually ... I'll lose. Thing is, I'm not into painful last stands, where I'm surrounded by a bunch of people when I trigger my armor's self-destruct. That's the way people like you and Patterson always want to go out."

"If you're not going to fight, then come with me. You'll be so happy."

"No thanks, Stacy. Just because I don't want to go out in a blaze of glory doesn't mean I want to sell myself into slavery. I may be a petty, two-bit criminal, but I plan on dying a free man. I'll at least go to my grave knowing that I didn't join up with the side that's ending human life as we know it."

"Stop it! You're not making any sense."

"...says the hero ready to run back to her supercrack. You're wasting valuable time, Stacy. You could be halfway up the escape ladder by now. Eternal bliss is just a few short steps away."

I start walking and she moves out of my way. Reaching the main control room, I interface with the computer and start going through the checklist to activate the base self-destruct. I see Stacy's reflection in the plasma monitor. "If you want to get back quicker, I think I can scare up a jetpack for you. The controls are pretty standard."

She continues to stare at my backside and limps toward the exit. Pausing, she says, "Are you sure you won't come?"

"Have a nice life, Stacy. Fair warning, I'll be playing Biz Markie shortly. I figure, a few more times for the road."

At the keypad, she punches in the first three numbers of Tommy Tutone's most famous song and stops. I follow her progress as she walks back down the steps and sits next to me.

"Do you need help getting to the surface?"

"Aphrodite ... the real one, pulled me aside on the day before we were leaving to come back from Olympus. She told me about all the things she did and the ones that she most regretted, cheating on her husband, warping, torturing, and sometimes killing people to satisfy her own vanity. She warned me not to follow in her path and hoped that I would bring honor and a measure of redemption to her name. I climb that ladder right now, and I'll know, deep down, I'm not living up to the one thing she asked of me."

"So you're going to stay?"

"Unless you can't cancel the self-destruct."

"That would be ironic, wouldn't it? But we're good. I was waiting until you got to the surface."

She gives me a weak smile, "My other condition for staying is that you don't play that damn song again – ever."

"If it means saving the world, I'm sure Biz would understand."

I go get the first aid kit. She pops four pain relievers while I tend to her scrapes and injuries.

"What do we do now?" she asks.

"I was hoping you'd know. Any idea where they have all the android and robot heroes in storage?"

"I've got a few guesses. We're still only two against the world." She winces a bit. The side of her face that I pressed into the wall is going to have some nasty bruises.

"Yeah, but those psi powers of yours, they aren't just psychokinetic, right? You can do something similar to what those bugs do?"

"Yes, except there's only one of me."

"I can fix the cells and we can capture a few other supers. With you around, we might have a chance of rehabbing them quicker."

"You mean without the lies and mind games."

"Sorry about that. I use what tools I have available. If we get enough of us together, we should be able to come up with a master plan." I try to make nice with her. I'm sorry I put her through it, but only after the fact. If we do try to rehab some of the other supers, I'll probably end up doing the same shit all over again.

"So you want to open a detox clinic? You're not exactly the nurturing type, trust me. Was I that much fun?"

"No, but we need more firepower. *And* a chance to come up with some kind of free-the-world scheme. While I fix the cells, you rest up and think of who we should try to grab."

Stacy nods, "I'm going to need something to protect me when we're up on the surface."

"We'll, I'm no Lazarus Patterson, but I've been known to make a set of armor or two. I should be able to rig something that'll keep the bugs out, give you flight and more protection, but still let you use your psi-bolts. It won't necessarily be the prettiest set of armor."

"Tell me about it."

"Easy on the sarcasm there, Aphrodite."

She chokes on the glass of water I gave her to wash down the pills. "You called me Aphrodite."

"You started acting like a hero again. Wait here, I'll get one of the spare rooms set up as a bedroom for you to use."

Just to be safe, I change the code on the keypad at the exit and set an alarm in case she tries to use the door.

Chapter Three

Like I Need Another Reason to Invade Branson, Missouri

We travel at night, a few hundred miles from "The Pig Sty." Cloud cover is good, and we're seeing whole sections of cities being converted into factories.

Aphrodite's armor is a hodgepodge of the previous Mark I and Mark II suits. Technically, it's the Mark II point one. I was forced to leave it light on the synth-muscle, but her superhuman strength compensates for it. Since she already has her own mode of attack, I gave the suit a single force blaster for a backup weapon and reserved most of the energy in the suit for shielding and maneuverability.

My com channel crackles to life. Aphrodite's insistent voice is on the other end. "Okay where is it?"

"It's not like I come up here to the Ozarks all the time. They stopped using me as a supplier three years ago and these storage depots aren't exactly meant to be found. It's a cave on the side of a mountain. Frankly, I'm lucky I remembered which mountain I used to deliver pulse cannons to."

Forty-five minutes later we're looking at a chamber full of inactive robot foot soldiers. My access code doesn't work, but good old Paul, the guy who cut me as a supplier, never removed my deceased girlfriend's code from the system. The robots are standard Type A fodder – the kind found in bases all over the world. It makes me wonder what poor son of a bitch got screwed out of his patents and designs for these robogrunts.

"Now comes the fun part. Put your hand at the back of each head, start a power transfer to get the rudiments of its operating system up and then install our command rootkit in the var directory."

"These things run on Linux?"

"Yeah, wouldn't want to have to wait around while your security force finishes blue screening. Still, this version is pretty old. If we were going to keep them, I'd recommend we upgrade it to the newest distribution, but since these things are going to get destroyed anyway…"

There's a hint of malice in her voice. "You're only programming them to attack the empty warehouses and to defend against super powered attackers."

"If I was Lazarus Patterson, would you be asking the same question?"

"He's not a criminal."

"That depends on your point of view. Try asking that to anyone who ever tried to patent their intellectual property after leaving his employment. What boggles my mind is how half the parts in these robots came from his factories and everyone believes he's a saint."

"Bitter with envy isn't a good look for you, Calvin. What about all those weapons that you built? *I'm sure they never hurt anyone.* Unlike you, he only sells to legitimate governments."

"…and turns a blind eye when they resell it. Exhibit A is lined up in rows in front of you." Great, there's no way I'm going to win this argument. She's not only an Ultraweapon fangirl, she's actually dated him.

"Oh, so some people using his technology for crime completely wipes out all the good he's ever done and, at the same time, it gives you carte blanche to excuse yourself for every gun you've ever built and sold in some back alley to a guy with no neck and a couple of dollars. You should listen to yourself sometime, hypocrite."

Tonight is looking like it's going to be a long one. She's more irritable when we're outside and she's locked inside her armor. I know she's thinking about the bugs. There's no one else to take it out on other than little old me.

Wisely, I concede and change the subject. "Fine, you're right. I'm a small-minded, petty criminal jealous of his success. Let's just drop it. Who do you think we're going to attract when we send these guys into the city?"

"Hopefully, they'll send some of the Olympians and we can grab one of my teammates."

I bite back my sarcasm and move on to the next robot. Aphrodite is looking to save her friends first. I'd prefer we start with a few mid-tier crime fighters rather than aiming for the proverbial brass ring. We actually discussed hunting down some of the bad guys, but odds were that we would end up fighting them as well. I'll be the token bad guy on this team, thank you very much.

There's a lot I wouldn't mind taking from here, but I'm limited by space – like going into a grocery store, where everything is free, but only getting one of those hand baskets that have to be carried instead of a shopping cart.

"The sooner we get these bots reprogrammed, the sooner we'll find out. Plus, there are a couple of spools of synth-muscle. I can finish wiring your armor up right."

"I still can't believe that someone went to the trouble of hiding a robot army near Branson, Missouri. Why would anyone want to attack a vacation destination?"

"You don't think like a villain, probably a good thing. You could send them here to draw the military in this direction while you attack Fort Leonard Wood, or Whiteman Air Force Base, or pick any place nearby. Of course, there's always the money in that city."

Stacy steps out from the row that she's working on. It's funny how she can make armor that I've worn for years, albeit with a few modifications, sexy. "It's always about the money isn't it?"

"Usually, it's the people with the money that are always screwing me over. But yeah, it's about the money probably seventy-five percent of the time. This is taking longer than I'd thought. We might as well take a break."

"Why?"

"At the rate we're going, it'll be almost morning before we finish and we won't be rested. I'd rather attack in the evening and be able to use the darkness to escape. The rainclouds will also help cover us."

"Just when I thought that your base was the absolute worst pit on the planet, you bring me here. How exactly do you sleep in this contraption?"

"Sit down and put your back against the wall. I've gotten used to it. There's music and some movies on your hard drive, if you don't feel like chatting." On a whim, I walk over to the small and lonely looking desk and pull open the drawers. A bitter laugh comes out of my mouth.

"What are you doing?" Aphrodite walks up behind me and looks down. "It's just a couple of trashy romance novels. What's so important about them?"

"They're Vicky's. She used to keep a supply of them around in these places when waiting for a delivery."

There's a slight teasing in her voice. "Why Cal, I didn't know you have a girlfriend."

"I don't. She's dead. One of the bodies they pulled out of Omega Base."

"Oh, I'm sorry ... I didn't mean to ..."

"Save it! I'm going offline to rest. I recommend you do the same." I dismiss her, probably rudely, and break off communications.

Even D-List supervillains have lives and things that once meant something to them. It isn't always about the money.

• • •

I've never led an army of robots attacking a city. It's a rush! No wonder people like Devious and Overlord get their jollies off of it. The arm mounted light pulse cannons riddle the empty but pristine buildings with holes, turning it into Swiss cheese, and within a minute or two it becomes so much rubble as my minions move on to the next completely identical structure. A few hours of uninterrupted rest and some gratuitous mayhem can do wonders to improve my mood.

Six factories later, I'm starting to get a bit bored when the first defenders finally show up. Response time is way down these days. Bullets start pinging off my armor and I spot several police officers. Calmly, I walk through the gunfire and arrive at the first officer while she reloads – no sense of preservation whatsoever. It's sad, but right now, I've got the better drones. Just like pulling a tick off of the family hunting dog, I reach out with my hand and pull the thing off of her neck. Clenching my fist, it turns into a greasy smear in my gauntlet.

The woman's eyes become unfocused and she collapses in a screaming mess. I step over her as the others begin firing and turn on my external microphone. "Unit Two, kill their bugs."

Mentioning her name might bring way too many superheroes running, so we'll play robots instead of people in armor. Her mental bolts start frying the insects. Some actually detach and start fleeing, leaving their hosts screaming. It's tempting to gloat, but instead I divert a few of the robots and grab the discarded weapons. Just because Stacy didn't attempt suicide doesn't mean these guys and gals won't.

Behind the policemen are just regular people armed with whatever they could grab. This could get real ugly, real fast. Aphrodite's bolts drop a bunch in their tracks as I do my best not to permanently injure them. "Save your energy. Let the suit do the work for you."

"But, I might hurt them," she protests over our internal frequency.

"You'll need your strength when the supers get here. Don't argue."

Long minutes pass and hundreds of bugs die along with people receiving assorted bruises and broken bones, but suddenly the throngs turn and begin to walk or crawl away in a most orderly fashion. That can only mean one thing.

"Here they come!" Aphrodite gestures to the tiny flame in the otherwise misty night. It's Apollo's chariot and probably most of her old team.

"All robots, attack the Olympians!" Wow! That sure does sound cheesy.

My reluctant teammate calls out a warning, "Heads up, Hermes is coming in fast."

The speedster tears through a pack of slow moving drones, smashing them with her metal rod. The mud is slowing her down a little, but she's making a beeline straight for me. I fire my pulse rifle at the ground separating us, spraying the wet earth in her way. A messy, muddy, and hopefully blind mass comes hurtling out of the plume of muck at high-speed, careening recklessly. I trigger the destruct sequence on the three nearest bots and let the shockwave knock her around a bit.

There's no time to waste and I lumber over to Hermes and snatch her into the air. She lashes out with her rod and I take dozens of hits on my helmet and chest piece. Her legs bludgeon me with jackhammer-like kicks. *Fifty amp defensive jolt!* We're briefly illuminated in a flash. It won't hurt the Olympian too much, but the bug on her is toast. Correction, make that bugs. There were three of them on her. That says loads about her metabolism.

"Stacy! I got one. Knock her out!" It takes two shots before the Olympian stops struggling. I toss Hermes to the ground, because I have a bigger problem and his name is Ares.

With my pulse rifle out of reach, thanks to Hermes, I hit him with my single force blaster. It barely slows the God of War down. Pulling my power sledge out, I meet him head on. The weapon's force field flares on impact. Ares screams but lowers his shoulder and bowls me over. We wrestle for a moment. His fists pound into my suit. Even through the armor, I can feel it. He rips my sledge from my grasp and raises it up. I shove my left palm into his face. *Fire force blaster!*

The sledge falls and I hit him with a right cross, while rerouting some of the remaining bots. I'm not the only one who'll be hating life tomorrow. Of course, he'll have much better drugs. Two robots blast him off of me and try to slow him down. He rips them to pieces, but it gives me the time to snatch the sledge off the ground and really clean his clock. I knock his ass at least twenty feet backwards.

To my disbelief, he starts to get back up. Holy shit, he's tough! I don't have time to process it as darkness becomes light. Apollo's fireball washes over me. Heat seeps through the cracks in my armor and I scream. I trigger my jetpack and dodge the second one. Landing, I grab my rifle. It still has enough charge for eight more shots, or I can overload it and chuck it at Apollo and Ares.

I like that idea. Five seconds and a massive explosion later, Ares is down a second time and doesn't look to be getting up. Apollo's in bad shape too – worse after I shoot him, twice. Staggering forward, I see Aphrodite fighting with Hera and Athena. Hermes gets another shot from my force blaster, for good measure. Hera's force fields keep stopping Stacy's psi-bolts while Athena's energy spears keep my partner in crime on the defensive.

Hera will never let me get close enough to use my sledge. Just like those old cartoons, I get a light over my head. In this case, the light is attached to a long metal pole and seconds later that streetlight is ripped out of the ground. Sometimes technology is overrated.

I pound away into the force field and allow Aphrodite a chance to go on the attack. "Quit screwing around and take her out."

"She's my friend! I don't want to hurt her."

I take a break from trying to bring down Hera's protective sphere and shoot "her friend" in the back with my force blaster, knocking her to the ground. Stacy finally gets the message and lays some smackdown on her party buddy.

Out of nearly two hundred drones, there are nine still functioning. My armor is a bit worse for wear after only a minute or two with Ares. Fortunately, I get to go back to the drawing board. I assign four robots to keep Hera entertained and the others to make sure that Apollo's chariot won't be able to fly anytime soon.

"We can't take Ares or Apollo. There's no way the cells will hold them. Hera is going to take too long. It's down to the speedster or the Goddess of Wisdom. Which one do we take?"

"Both."

"Two? You were hard enough by yourself and you know how quickly the speedster is going to eat all our food."

"It won't be a problem. I'll take care of both of them. You won't notice a thing."

Why do I feel like she's asking me for two puppies instead of one?

• • •

Stacy comes in to the workshop on the morning of the third day after our raid. "Cal?"

"Yes," I stop winding the artificial muscles into progressively tighter bundles. The denser it is the better. My suit held up against Hermes, Ares, and Apollo, but just barely. The pulse rifle wasn't all I hoped it would be and I'm addressing that.

The good news is that Stacy has been marginally nicer to me since we captured her friends. With her new "project," she's too busy to sit around and complain about how awful my base is.

"I got a little distracted trying to talk sense into Holly and Keisha ... well, um ... where do you keep the bucket?"

I savor the look of frustration on her face. "Interface with the palm pad at the base of the steps, it's in the closet there. How are you at installing toilets?"

"How do you think? That's the other reason I'm here. Gloating doesn't suit you."

I finish off the strand of muscle that I was working on and grab my helmet. "I'm not gloating. I'm truly enjoying this."

"Look, I've barely had any sleep and the only thing keeping them from going batshit is my psionic powers. All I'm asking for is a little bit of help. Please?"

It's tempting to make her beg, but I'm not that heartless. "Yeah, I'll take a four hour shift with the girls. Why don't you get some sleep?"

Aphrodite gives me a thankful smile and says, "I just can't believe how mean the two of them are. Holly actually asked me if my new haircut meant that I was a dyke. They're supposed to be my friends!"

"That's just the withdrawal symptoms talking. Even with your psychic whammy, they're still hurting. Have you managed to get anything useful out of them yet?"

"If you count Keisha giving me a detailed list of anatomical suggestions, most of which are impossible, then yes. If not, no. I'm beginning to wish that you really had tanks of knockout gas."

I shrug, while she mutters about how she fell for that one. "It's never easy is it? Just go get some rest and I will handle this problem. Do you happen to know what music they really hate?"

Stacy winces, knowing what's going to happen, "Keisha hates classical music with a passion. I've never heard Holly say that she hates any particular brand of music."

"Which do you think I should start with Wagner's *Flight of the Valkyries*, or perhaps a tribute to the great Ludwig Van? It worked in Kubrick's movie."

"What?"

Oh, she did not just ask that! "Never mind. The white noise generator should keep it from bothering you."

"What have you been doing up here? New version of the suit?"

"I'm that predictable?"

"Yes. What was so wrong with the last one?"

"The rifleman version was good for medium to long distance fighting. Ares got me into close combat and I don't want to count on dumb luck again."

Stacy affects an air of interest. "Rifleman version? What's this version going to be called?"

"Screaming Cyclops. I'm keeping my hands free and moving the single force blaster into the larger helmet. If I simplify the arms and legs, there's less of a chance of things going wrong and more room for extra muscle and shield modules. I'm adding a shoulder mounted grenade launcher for concussion grenades."

She leans over the schematics and I become acutely aware of her presence. "Okay, I get the Cyclops part. What makes it screaming?"

"The thorax has a variable frequency generator in it?"

"That's a fancy way of saying that you copied the Bugler isn't it?"

"Um..."

Now she's genuinely laughing, "After all the bitching you've been doing about the Biloxi Bugler, you're copying him?"

"It's not how it looks! ... Okay, it is how it looks, but sonic weapons have a much lower power consumption rate and it makes an effective secondary weapon that doesn't take up much space."

"If you say so. Are you making a new rifle then?"

I gesture to the six disassembled pulse pistols and the long cylinder. "I'm going to combine those into a Gatling configuration for medium to short range firepower. I'll trade stopping power for rate of fire and still keep energy consumption down."

"Sounds like it will work. Good luck with that. Thanks for giving me a break. Don't be too hard on them, they're my friends."

I'm shocked at her encouragement, she must be tired. "Get some rest, Stacy."

A few minutes later, I am indulging in the most useless waste of time ever. I'm listening to an addict rant. Holly Crenshaw is supposedly a level-headed woman – the Goddess of Wisdom. Hell, she's led the Olympians almost as much as Hera.

In between the usual insults, she tries to go after me about Stacy. "You know this is the only way you'll ever have a shot with her, Stringel."

"You're a lousy addict, Crenshaw. Of course I don't have a chance."

She frowns seeing that I'm not biting and then offers up a new tactic, "But you could with me."

"No thanks, Holly. That didn't work when Stacy was in there and we both know she's way better looking than you. Besides, in a couple days you are going to smell pretty fresh unless you start taking care of some basic hygiene. Your kind offer will lose a good deal of its appeal by then."

Aphrodite's psionic powers are helping them cope as they come off the bug juice and both are more coherent than Stacy was. It doesn't stop them from being bitches, but their rants at least make more sense.

She summons an energy spear and hurls it against the walls, protected by a force field generator. It's creating a strain on my base's power supply, but things are okay for the moment. With any luck, Hermes will detox in a few days because of her freakish metabolism. Three watching one beats two on two any day of the week.

"You should cut Aphrodite some slack. She's trying to save you. If it was up to me, I'd have picked Hermes and just left you. After all, you're not really much of a leader, are you? You and the rest of the heroes let the world get overrun. Face it, Crenshaw, which one of us is the real loser?"

I walk away from her cell while mentally patting myself on the back. The great and mighty Athena needs some help hitting rock bottom and I am only too happy to assist. Thirty feet later, I'm at Keisha St. Croix's cell. I don't have a force field generator on this one and the walls and door are already showing the effects of her sustained blows. I keep a white noise generator running so neither of the two prisoners can communicate.

Instantly, she appears at the small opening. Tiny slivers of porcelain from the shattered toilet fly through the crack and ricochet off my helmet.

"Cute. Ineffective as hell, but still cute. I brought you a bucket for when you need to go poopies."

"Better say your prayers now, metal man. I will make sure your death is so fast you won't even know what hit you!"

"No, I was stopping by to thank you. Beneath the concrete and metal of the floor and walls is a layer of kinetic receptors. All that running around you are doing and all that pounding on the walls, it's helping to power my base. Considering how much you eat, I just wanted you to know that you are least earning your keep."

She snarls at me and begins yelling so fast and so profanely that I could swear there were ten comedians in there, all telling their nastiest jokes at the same time. I wish I had kinetic receptors in the floor and all kinds of other cool toys, but sometimes a lie is just as effective. The funny thing is that they keep right on believing me. Their cravings make them gullible and their ego reinforces the fact that no mere prison cell can hold them.

I decide to see how far I can push this. "Listen, Keisha ... can I call you that? Anyway, I'm probably going to have to turn one of you two loose. I could probably be talked into letting you go if you've got some useful information. Otherwise, it'll probably end up being Athena who gets to go back to the bugs. She's been a fountain of information."

Hermes screams in rage, "Let me go! I'll tell you whatever you want to know."

"Where are all the android heroes being held?"

"Go to hell!"

"Aw c'mon Keisha, it's just you and me. You can tell me where those guys are. In fact, I just happen to have something you *really* want."

I pull out a plastic case and hold it up to let her see. Inside of it there's a bug moving around. I'm guessing Stacy wouldn't approve of this technique – too bad she's not here.

Keisha starts talking. She doesn't stop for almost ten minutes, before refusing to say anything else until she gets the bug.

Smiling, I open the service hatch and drop it in to the bucket. Interfacing with the cell door control, I open her side. She whips the box inside and frantically opens the top. I'm already turning down my external microphones as screams of anguish emanate from her prison. I should feel bad using a holographic chip to trick her like that, but I don't.

Instead, I start casually back towards Athena's cell and grab the other holographic bug box, so I can get some independent verification. Activating the music system, I pull up a file of somebody's Philharmonic Orchestra doing Beethoven's greatest hits. I hope she enjoys the concert. After I get done with Holly, I think she should learn to appreciate speedmetal.

Someone famous once said, "War makes good people do bad things." If that's the case, it also makes bad people even worse.

Chapter Four

Free Choice and Other Stellar Ideas

"Thank you for reactivating me," Andydroid says.

"Two … well technically three victories in a row," I answer. I'll try not to let it go to my head, but I do think it's a personal best."

Andydroid is an interesting robot. He's got far more personality installed than any other mechanical construct I've been around. His creator was a partner for a time with Patterson's grand pappy back in the day, but they had a falling out over the old quality versus quantity argument and parted ways. Promethia started churning out Type A robots as fast as it could to get into the mechanical arms race while the reclusive Mister Albright went the other way making robot heroes like Andy, the Cyber Dudes, and the Silicon Sisterhood were programmed to avoid taking life where possible and use logic to solve situations rather than brute force.

"Still, the act requires gratitude, so I give it."

"We're going to need all the help we can get and it's good that you and the Dudes are immune. Too bad about the Sisterhood though," I say wondering if there's a robot heaven or some kind of great scrap heap in the sky. All that was left of them when we raided that warehouse were a bunch of spare parts and most of that went to getting the Cyber Dudes operational.

"I'm just glad you guys don't eat anything the way Hermes is running through my stores."

"What would you like me to do?" Andydroid asks.

I like him more and more by the second. He's a giver and not a taker – unlike the two recently rehabbed Olympians. They're just a pair of bitches no matter what Stacy says. I'd throw them back in the cells, but we picked up a couple of super powered prisoners while liberating our new allies and I use the term super powered loosely. Over my protests, we brought back Rodentia and Gunk. The pair of minor villains hadn't been useful for anything other than guard duty.

Here I thought all the rehabbing females developed nasty hygiene problems. These guys were questionable even before the bugs and no one was prepared for excessive amounts of body hair and mucus, but hey, Rodentia can summon a legion of tiny rodents and Gunk can ... well, he spits and that cell is getting downright nasty. Clearly having them on our side tilts the balance of power, but I just can't come up with a use for them other than to convert oxygen to carbon dioxide.

"Andy, I appreciate you keeping an eye on the prisoners," I say. "You probably want to put on a protective suit anyway. That crap Gunk spits is hard to get off and might damage your finish."

"Consider it done."

He leaves and I turn my attention to my other problem. Her name is Athena. Now free, she's gone from an annoying nuisance to a genuine pain in the ass. We butt heads on a routine basis. Andy isn't gone fifteen minutes before she comes in and gets up in my face.

"Stringel! Who said you could task Andydroid? Where the hell is your inventory? I need to know what you have, how much you have, and I need to know it now."

Athena looks impatient while Aphrodite lingers in the doorway trying to decide if she needs to play peacekeeper.

"I think it's around here somewhere." I fish around on my desk for a moment. Coming up with a clipboard, I toss it to her.

She looks down at the pad of paper attached. "It's blank."

"Oh right, here's a pen. Let me know if you can't access any of the storage closets, Holly. I might have a couple of them still restricted."

"What kind of shitty fly by night operation have you got here, Stringel?"

I almost fall back on the backup base excuse, but frankly I'm tired of her griping and respond, "The same one that rescued you. You want an inventory, have at it or delegate it to your speedster and the other androids. I'm busy."

With a nasty glare, she says, "It'd go faster if you pitch in. As you're so fond of reminding me, this is your shithole."

"Well let's see, I could stop working on these concussion grenades and trying to figure out something that we can use to protect Hermes without weighing her down too much, but I don't think so. Even though I've been dying to know how many rectal thermometers I have, I'll just let someone else tell me. You want it done, feel free. Don't forget to add the stick up your ass to the list. That'll come in handy, I'm sure."

She storms out in anger. Beneath my helmet I'm grinning. Sometimes, embracing my pettiness is the best course of action.

"You should try to get along with her. She's under a lot of stress." Stacy says, walking into my workshop. She's out of her armor and wearing a very loose set of coveralls. Amazingly enough, all the spare clothing inside this base was bought to fit me.

"And I'm not? She should be a bit more grateful. You want to know what I think. She's pissed because a 'nobody' like me is responsible for saving her ass."

Her lips purse tightly. "You're not a 'nobody.' Don't say that. Just do me a favor and try to get along with her. We need her tactics as much as we need your firepower. Right now, you're our heavy hitter."

"That doesn't really say much for you guys."

She slaps my shoulder, "Quit. I've seen you take out a good portion of my team including some of the most powerful around. Technically, you're two and oh against the Olympians."

"You're forgetting that the first one was a poorly executed trap. The second one? Well, they were a bunch of brainwashed zombies and we had two hundred robots to slow them down. Don't go promoting me to the big leagues just yet."

"I'll be back in a minute. Wait right here."

I start to say, 'Where the hell else would I go?' but I choke it back. Curious, I tap into the base feed and follow her as she goes to the room she shares with Athena and watch her pull some familiar books from the dresser. What is she doing with those?

She brings Vicky's old tawdry romance books back with her. "I grabbed these at that storage depot. They were your girlfriend's right?"

I'm somewhat choked up for reasons I can't quite fathom. "Yeah. Have you been reading them?"

"When I'm bored," she says and laughs, "Even the Goddess of Love needs an occasional inspiration, but you should have them."

"I'm more of a technical manual kind of guy. Keep them and enjoy them. It's a nice gesture. I appreciate it."

"You're welcome. I'll speak to Athena and tell her to back off. I'm going to go help her with that inventory, but afterwards can you walk me through some of the maintenance on my armor?"

"Is something wrong? I can fix it."

"No, but down the road, I might need to fix it when you're not around. I'm thinking of buying it off of you after all this is over."

"Really?"

She grins, "I've always been considered one of the weaker Olympians, yet there I was holding my own against Hera and Athena at the same time. A gal could get used to that. So, you mind showing me some of the basics?"

"Uh, sure."

"Thanks. I'll come by this evening." She walks off and I focus on the gentle sway of her bottom as she heads out the door.

Okay, I'm officially confused as hell.

• • •

On the security cameras, I follow her back to her room. She pulls Athena in and I turn up the volume.

"Holly, damnit! Do you have to be such a bitch to him? I know you're still coming off that bug juice, but give him a break."

"Why are you defending him? He's not even a 'has been,' more like a 'never was.' Ultraweapon could run circles around him."

I wince. Stacy glares at her friend. "Cal's a lot sharper than you give him credit for. Do you really think Lazarus, without all his engineers and resources, would be that much better? Cut Cal some slack. He's actually a decent guy and he's obviously got some self-esteem issues. You're not making things better."

Somewhat stunned at her proclamation, I barely catch Athena asking, "How so?"

"Ever see him completely out of his armor? He'll take off the gauntlets and maybe the helmet while he's working, but I've been here for nearly six weeks and he's always in it."

Athena seems unimpressed. "He's a liability. How many times have we worked with the bad guys only to have them screw us at some critical point? Tell me one time that it's worked out? That's right! I thought so."

"Look, he didn't do this. He's a real person too. Even after he let me out, up until we brought you and Keisha back, I was treating him the same way you are right now. I stopped before you got out of the cells when I saw Keisha doing it too. Cal needs some encouragement."

"If you really want to make him feel better, you'll do what you usually do, Stacy, jump his bones a few times. That's the way you've handled things ever since we met."

There's an awkward moment of silence before Athena speaks up again. "Shit! I'm sorry, Stacy. I didn't mean to say that. I'm still not right."

Aphrodite wipes a tear from her eye. "Do you need another pick me up?"

Athena nods her head and I watch Stacy's aura flare. A tendril of energy flicks out and Athena's expression softens as a delirious smile spreads across her face.

"Thanks I needed that. You might have overdone it. Now, I'm horny."

"In that case, maybe you should be the one jumping his bones," Stacy laughs.

Crenshaw makes a face. "Not likely. He's better than the guys in the cells, but not by much. I wonder if Andy is anatomically correct."

"You're awful! So can you play nice with Cal? C'mon Holly, give him a chance. I'm not taking any static from you."

"I'll try, but he's still a prick. I do not have a stick up my ass."

Aphrodite really laughs. "Yes, you do. Now let's go see how many rolls of toilet paper he has in this dump."

"Hey, you just called it a dump!"

"It is, but you don't have to rub his face in it."

• • •

Her comment about static got me thinking. The result is a belt with a large buckle around St. Croix's waist. Hermes is looking at it skeptically.

"It looks like something a rapper or a bull rider would wear."

"Armor will slow you down, but this belt has a base charge and as you move it will recharge. Mind touching her, Athena?"

They touch and there's a decent electrical shock that both shrug off. "Big deal, I'm a human joy buzzer."

"You're both Olympians. That's more than enough juice to kill any bug landing on you. The wires going up to the rubber gloves, they carry a bigger shock that you can use without zapping yourself."

My self-appointed cheerleader jumps in, "That's pretty clever, isn't it?"

The Cyber Dudes seem to like it and Andy helped me flesh out the design. He and I actually get along. Considering my other idea was putting her into some kind of giant hamster ball and turn her into a human pinball. The belt idea was more workable. Plus, I didn't have enough plastic to make the ball. Too bad, it would have been epic.

I'm also working on a pair of electrified brass knuckles to use on the Cyclops suit. The synth-muscle can only amplify my punch so much, so I'll have to cheat the next time I encounter a strongman and I can cheat with the best of them.

Athena renders her judgment, "It's usable. Good job, Stringel. As soon as you finish those weapons for the androids, we can try to get some of the others liberated. Alright, has anyone come up with an idea to get rid of the bugs?"

Andy speaks up in his digitized voice, "I have completed my analysis of their physiology from the carcasses we brought back when I was rescued. The creatures are fairly resistant to both radiation and chemical attacks. To be effective, we would be forced to use them in quantities that would result in death for the host. That option is not the optimal solution."

It's sobering news. I look at it logically. "Why don't we try to go to the Overlord's base? He's bound to have something that lets him control these things."

"We can't. Ultraweapon destroyed his base. These things escaped when that happened. If there was something there to control them, it's gone now."

"You're shitting me! Lazarus Patterson is responsible for all this?" A tiny part of me delights in that news.

Stacy speaks trying to defend him, "That's the report we got. Anyway, I can kill them easily enough, but my range is too limited, I could probably do a football field in size, maybe a square mile if I went all out."

Athena ponders the idea. "If we could boost your power some, it might be more effective. What about that throne thing that General Devious uses? It boosts her power. Do you know where her current base is, Stringel?"

She's obviously mistaken me for someone higher up on the food chain. "I've got a vague idea, but it's not like there's a Supervillain's edition of the phonebook."

Hermes, still looking over her belt, cuts off the fight before it starts. "Don't we have one of the old versions in our vault at Mount Olympus?"

"They've changed our codes by now. Do we really want to try to attack our headquarters? No one's ever succeeded."

"You got a better idea?"

I'm a little more practical, "What other goodies do you have stashed in your vault? If we're going shopping for gadgets, why don't we figure out if it's even worth going there."

Taking notes, I'm treated to the greatest adventures of the Olympians as they talk about all the villainous paraphernalia in their headquarters. I'm surprised how many of these adventures I've never heard before. Then again, we villains don't exactly get together and talk about how badly we just got our ass handed to us. I start asking questions about the capabilities of the devices they have in their base.

Hours later, I'm standing alone in my workshop looking at dozens of little note cards spread out on the table. It's a jigsaw puzzle of how to save the human race. The only problem is that I'm not sure I have all the pieces. Crenshaw has already stopped by to see if I had anything, only to be turned away disappointed. What was she expecting? I don't shit out miracles on demand! I scribble two more note cards, one for mind control and the other for power boosting and start sorting all over again.

Assuming we get our hands on The General's throne, and it works, it'll give Stacy a big boost – maybe five or ten square miles at a time. The next problem would be protecting her as we travel all across the world. That would be in addition to trying to care for all addicts that were suddenly missing their fix.

"Are you doing okay, Cal? You haven't come out in hours." Stacy asks after knocking on my doorframe.

Smacking one of my hands on the table, I sigh. "I can't come up with anything that's going to work on the scale we need it to."

"No one's expecting you to solve it all by yourself. Why don't you take a break?"

"Has Athena said we need to start targeting Lazarus and his scientists yet?"

"Um, no."

"You're not a very good liar, Stacy."

She shrugs. It's incredible just to watch her do it. "Okay, she has, but don't let that get you down. You've done an awful lot here, but Lazarus is an organizational genius. This kind of thing is up his alley."

"Of course there's one hitch, where in the world is Lazarus Patterson? The bugs are probably using his so-called creative genius rather than his Ultraweapon suit."

"We're thinking we could track him with his Blackberry if he's still carrying it. You know, figure out what cell phone tower his phone is responding to and then track him down."

The thought of him sitting in a cubicle somewhere, for sixteen hours a day, designing weapons that no one is going to build amuses me. Still, I'm about to be kicked to the curb. Obscurity, it's just a phone call away.

Wait a damn second! "Cell towers! That's it!"

Aphrodite is confused. "What are you talking about?"

I fish around through the cards until I find the combination. "I've only been focusing on the things in your vault. The delivery system is already in place. I just didn't think of it until now. The General's chair will boost your power right?"

"Well yeah, but we've been through this before. It's not enough."

"Unless we use The Wireless Wizard's dead zone gear and use the cell phone towers all across the world to carry your signal. His stuff would use the cell towers and people's own mobile phones as weapons. We don't have to lug you and the chair all around the world. We can just have a big old bug killing teleconference! There's The Overlord's Mindwiper too. The energy might not be able to go through the Wizard's gear, but if we hit the heroes with the ray and wipe out the last three months worth of memories, they'll still have the cravings and feel like shit, but won't remember why."

She runs it through her mind. "It's brilliant! I'll get Holly."

Of course, there is the small matter of breaking into the Olympian's headquarters – the most secure location in the world. It'll be just like a big bank job, a piece of cake, right? Oh wait; I never had much luck with banks.

• • •

"So, are you ready for tomorrow?" Stacy asks, using a diagnostic scanner on her suit as I watch.

"Ready as I can be, I guess. It's nice that you're really serious about your armor. Crenshaw just wants her suit to work."

"I'd watch Lazarus working on his when we dated. Anytime I'd ask questions, he'd get really possessive. It was kind of strange considering he usually had an entire team of techs working on it at any given time."

"You weren't on his payroll. Either way, his suit is a corvette and mine's a dump truck. Plus, I'm used to people giving my stuff the once over. It's generally haggling over the price that irritates me."

Rolling her eyes, she chuckles. "Given any thought to what you'll do after all this is over, Cal?"

"Well, I'll have to get a new base. Everyone knows where this one is." I don't bother mentioning that should we lose, I'll be welcoming my insect overlords with open arms.

"You could always play for the good guys. I'd vouch for you. The Guardians pay their heroes."

I pick up a piece of metal on the bench and flex it in my hands nervously. "Me? Punching the clock and picking up a paycheck, bankrolled by Uncle Sam and Promethia? I don't see it. Plus, there's some bad blood between me and the guys here on the Gulf Coast."

She's trying to rehabilitate me. "Give it some thought. You keep saying how no one's ever given you a fair shake."

"We'll see how it plays out. What about you? If we win, you're going to be stuck on that throne playing 'Miss Twelve Step program' to a few billion people all going through withdrawal at the same time. That's going to be thrilling."

"Yeah, I'm trying not to think about it, but it's going to be even worse for you guys. I'll be safe in Headquarters and you'll be out there dealing with all the depressed and suicidal people. I'll take being inside over riot duty any day."

"Riot duty?" I check the list of things I've signed up for, that isn't on it.

"I'm guessing Athena hasn't spoken to you about this yet."

"That's a fair assumption."

"We're going to be so shorthanded after this that we're going to need everyone to pitch in."

"So you're recruiting me?"

"I figured you might need a bit of persuasion."

I mull it over. "I don't have any other plans. I'll do it, but only because it's you asking."

Stacy smiles at me and disconnects the scanner from her armor. "Good. I'm glad that's settled. Now, I'm going to go take a long hot shower and get cleaned up. Mind if I use the one in your bedroom?"

As I fumble for an answer, she sets the scanner on the workbench and laughs. "Funny, that's basically how we met isn't it?"

"Yeah, if I hadn't turned on the camera in the bathroom to record it we'd both be little drones right now."

"Do you have cameras in these showers?"

Inside my armor I gulp and stammer, "No, just in the main rooms and the cells."

"That's a shame. You could always bring a camcorder in and do it old school."

The world stops for a moment as I try to process what she just said. My climate control inside the suit seems to be failing. All I can manage to squeak out is, "Are you serious?"

"Yes. Tomorrow, we could die or worse, be turned into slaves. I want to do one last thing that's my choice, of my own free will, and I'm feeling the need to work off the pre-battle jitters. How about it, Cal?"

There's absolutely no arguing with that logic. Count me in!

Chapter Five

War Dialing FTW

This morning, I'm still trying to rationalize what happened. It couldn't have meant anything to her. It was just a diversion, merely something (or someone) to do. Though she said she was impressed because she reached what she calls, "the second level," something that doesn't happen that often. It's this *other* thing where she ends up venting some of her powers. All I can say about that is it got me right back in the game and both Holly and Keisha were giving her shit about it this morning because they caught some of the backlash. I try to push it aside and focus on the task at hand.

"Listen, you two are essential to our plan to raid Promethia. We can't pull it off without you." I say trying to sound sincere.

Gunk and Rodentia are lapping it up, just looking for a way out. They're nowhere near cured and that's exactly the point.

"Our team here will head out to Promethia's West Coast offices and our other team will assault the West Coast Guardians' base. We're certain they have a weapon there that will stop the bugs. Rodentia, we'll need lots of your furry creatures and Gunk, we need you to ... to start making mucus."

I finally came up for a use for these two losers – decoys. They will "escape" shortly and waste no time finding the nearest bugs. The bugs aren't deep thinkers and are probably bigger suckers for lies than the heroes. With any luck, most of their super-powered drones will be hours away on the west coast when we attack New Mount Olympus, outside of Washington DC. That's good, because we're going to need time to get this all to work.

One of the perks about being a bad guy is that I'm not above using people. It's doubtful that any of the heroes would've come up with this one, except Stacy. She's probably had a lot of experience using people. I've recently been added to that list, or maybe I'm jumping to conclusions. Either way, I need to stop thinking about her!

The reality is that we're stealing one of the Gulf Coast Guardians' planes and heading east.

Smiling inside my helmet, I give them the key code to open the outer door and say that we'll be letting them out of the cells shortly.

Returning to the control room, I say to the rest of the team, "It's done. All that's left is to set them loose."

Andydroid, Aphrodite, and I have the technical part of the mission, making the Wireless Wizard's equipment work with the throne. The rest have to protect us using whatever they can for as long as possible.

• • •

Amidst the hordes of Type B guard-bots, I fire my Gatling mini-gun wildly. Blasts of energy and concussion grenades strike my opponents indiscriminately. There is no shortage of targets. The Type B's aren't even humanoid; they're just rolling balls with heavy stun guns attached on rotating stabilizers. The bad guys usually equip them with something much more offensive, but the Olympians make up for it in quantity.

I use my jetpack and strafe them, swooping through the masses, cutting a path, and drawing fire away from my teammates. It's weird being part of a team and I'm trying to adjust to it.

Athena and Aphrodite are struggling with Poseidon. The Sea Lord's dense skin allows him to soak up their best attacks like a sponge. Super strength and high-pressure blasts of water keep them busy. Once Stacy killed his bug, it sent him into a berserker rage. She's probably regretting that now.

Hermes is holding her own against both Demeter and a squad of robots. Andydroid and the Cyber Dudes help me with the robots and the gun emplacements rising out of the ground. Landing, I feel the ground shake as a pair of Type D Warbots step out from the faux Greek columns surrounding the headquarters. The "Death Dealers" are coming up next. They're going to need massed firepower to beat and we're too spread out at the moment.

If we don't turn the tide soon, we might not even make it inside. This is the part where I usually run away – except I know that there's nowhere to left to run. I toss the mini-gun to Andy and trigger my jetpack. Accelerating into the backside of Poseidon, I slam him into one of the sculptures, trigger a full electrical discharge, and give him a helmet-mounted force blaster noogie. The power levels in the suit immediately begin dropping at the continuous release of energy.

It's everything I've got and I know it might not be enough. Pulling him into a full-nelson, I trigger my flight system and drag him skyward. If he can survive the crushing depths of the ocean, a big drop shouldn't kill him.

I manage only about a few hundred feet before Poseidon breaks my hold and nearly dislocates a shoulder. He twists and wraps an arm around my neck. I'm staring into his enraged face as his other arm cocks back a fist. Oh shit!

Activate sonic generator! Fire force blaster! Earmuffs clamp down a millisecond before the high decibel wail begins. It takes a second blast from the helmet gun before he lets go – my own version of "catch and release". I'd like to say that his plunge into a Type D Warbot was completely planned and perfectly executed, but it wasn't. It was luck, pure and simple. Either way, it's what we need.

I dive bomb the giant robot as Athena and Aphrodite hammer away at it. My weight hits its upper back, driving it down to the ground as its servos and stabilizers adjust to my sudden weight. I go right for the Poseidon-sized dent in the shoulder and start ripping armor plating away and firing into the inner workings. Sending my last two concussion grenades down the hole, I fly off and let the primary and secondary explosions rip it to pieces.

My shields protest against the blasts of the remaining turrets and the other Warbot. I'm swatted back down to the ground and rise out of a freshly made crater, already checking my diagnostics and firing my Cyclops blaster. Hurling chunks of the destroyed robot at its companion, I play kickball with a Type B.

That's strange, Athena and Hermes are still standing, but the Warbot is attacking me. Must be a glitch in the threat selection programming.

Faulty subroutines or not, it's one of the last things standing between us and the exterior of the Olympian's Headquarters. I reach for my sledgehammer and find it missing – lost during the fight somewhere. It doesn't matter.

Hermes zips up next to me and shoves the mini-gun in my hands. I feel her popping a fresh clip of twelve grenades into the launcher. Her face is bleeding and her voice is ragged, "Take it out and we're in!"

Backed by energy spears, force blasts, rockets, and a kitchen sink or two, I take flight and advance on the almost ten meter tall machine. Other than Ultraweapon's suit, it's the pinnacle of Promethia's technology. It's the next best thing to fighting Patterson himself and I've never been more eager in my life.

Less than a minute later, amidst ground shaking explosions, the huge robot topples into the side of the building and disintegrates in a flaming mass of destruction. I emerge from the wreckage and, for the first time, understand what I am truly capable of.

• • •

Inside the base, Hestia, the remaining Olympian, proves to be little trouble, but we know that she sent out the alarm. The clock is ticking. We're down to one fully-functional Cyber Dude and Andy. Hermes is looking downright awful as she speed-eats, replenishing her energy. Already two bugs have tried to land on her and suffered a shocking demise. Athena's damaged armor lies in a useless pile at her feet. She's dressing in thick clothes to protect her from the bugs.

I'm connecting fresh powercells from the Olympian's stock when Athena issues the orders. "Stacy, get Andy and Stringel into the vault. The rest of us will buy you time, so make it work!"

The Olympians' vault – for a technogeek like me, is like Christmas come early. I could spend a full week in here just looking around. The throne is easy to locate. Size and image matter a great deal to the General. I'm already running cable to the base power supply while Andy and Stacy search for the Wireless Wizard's telecommunications gear and the Overlord's Mindwiper.

The good news is that Hestia, who maintains the base, is an obsessive compulsive type. Each display is meticulously labeled. The bad news is that there are an awful lot of them. Athena and Hermes deploy the few remaining Type B robots to keep the normals out of the way, but when the big dogs get here, they'll make short work of them, and we've taken out all the other defenses.

"How's it coming?" Athena's voice comes over the announcing system, "We've already got incoming. Looks like WhirlWendy and a few other Guardians."

"The chair's powering up, maybe ten minutes before it's charged. Stacy's getting into the Wizard's suit. She's going to need time to figure out how to use it. Andy's still looking for the Mindwiper."

"I don't need to tell you that time is of the essence."

"You just did."

"Bite me, Stringel!"

"If you run out of energy spears, don't forget the stick. You can use that too!"

Athena breaks contact in a huff as Stacy glowers at me. She's trying to fit gracefully into a suit clearly made for a three hundred pound man, "Cal, what did I tell you?"

"I was only trying to be helpful and give her a fall-back strategy. Andy, while you're looking for the Mindwiper, see if you can find something using a standard power cable. The General's throne has a second interface. We can get it powered up faster with another cable."

"Don't ignore me, Cal."

"Sorry Stacy, there are people in this world who don't get along. Holly and I are two of those people."

She pauses for a moment, bunching up the fiber mesh of the suit and connecting it to the backpack with the satellite dish attached. "You do know that you're going to have to make a better effort to get along with my best friend if you're serious about being my boyfriend."

Despite the obvious danger of approaching superheroes and the time crunch surrounding us, that phrase stops me in my tracks. I sputter, "Come again?"

"Hopefully, yes," she grins at me.

"Are you serious?"

"Why not? But let's work out the details after this whole save the world thing, okay?"

Andy interrupts my stupor by shoving a power cable into my hands and I gather my scattered wits about me. I scramble to get the cable connected to the throne and load a code-breaker into the keypad. Given that they've had this chair for a few years; my cracker should break it in less than five minutes.

I'm off the chair and back by Stacy helping her with the backpack. "Looks like the interface is on the left wrist. Activate it and tell me what you see."

"It's mapping out the nearby sites for the Three-Oh-One and Two-Oh-Two Area Codes. Wow! I can use the cell towers to see, sort of. Oh no! Apollo's chariot is inbound."

"Andy! Get her in the chair. I've got a minicomputer attached to the keypad breaking the code. When it finishes, punch it in and lower the headgear. I'll go see if I can buy you a few minutes more."

Stacy looks worried. She motions for me to open my helmet. When I do, she leans in and kisses me. "Good luck, Cal."

I scoop up the mini-gun and head to the door. "I'm counting on you to save the day, Aphrodite. I'll concentrate on saving the next five minutes. Seal the door behind me."

Opening the door, I charge out, trying to banish childhood memories of Newman and Redford running out to fight the entire Bolivian Army.

The sight before me makes me wish for a plain old army – I might have a chance against that. Instead, I see Ares hoisting Athena over his head like a rag doll while some flying hero I don't recognize rips the clothes away with his claws. A swarm waits close by and a bug immediately jumps on Holly Crenshaw.

Hermes is still sprinting around, but she's slowing down and going to be overwhelmed any second now. Athena stops struggling and points an accusing hand at me. Oops! Someone just told everyone about our little scheme. I zero in on the crowd around Ares. *Fire all concussion grenades! Activate sonic generator!*

The high-pitched piercing whine and the detonations of forty millimeter grenades at least show that I'm going out with a bang. Maybe I should go e-mail the Spartans, because my last stand is going to be on the steps of Mount Olympus. I swivel the business end of my energy mini-gun around and cut loose.

"Eat hot plasma!" Of course no one can hear me over the sonic generator, but that's not the point. I concentrate my fire on the ones that come charging, heedless of the ear-splitting pain.

The crowd pushes me in through the opening where the doors once were. It actually works to my advantage, limiting the people who can kick my ass at any given time to only five or six. The mini-gun is ripped from my arms and I resort to flailing limbs, electrical discharges and bolts from my helmet blaster.

I stand my ground, giving much better than I'm getting, but it's like a bear being surrounded by wolves. I can't hold them for long! Shields begin to falter and an uppercut from a visibly bloody Ares sends me flying into the wall and triggers a warning klaxon in my ear.

Suit power at six percent! I fire the last shot from my helmet blaster and struggle to stay on my feet. It doesn't work. The view from down on my knees is better anyway.

That's it! I've done all I can. The heroes, most driven to the brink of sanity by the loss of their bugs, close in.

I'm watching my life flash before my eyes, trying to fast forward to get to the parts involving the love goddess when the doors behind me are blasted off their hinges. The hairs on the back of my neck rise as the air around me crackles with power.

A bolt of energy washes down the hallway over my head knocking everyone back. Andy comes out with what must be the Mindwiper in his hands and starts zapping everyone in sight. He drops a pair of fresh powercells at my feet.

The energy boost gets me back up to thirty-five percent, allowing me to bypass damaged systems. Standing, I cast a glance over my shoulder and see Stacy. She's bathed in light and glowing like the goddess she truly is. I stumble forward and grab the mindwiped Ares.

He opens his eyes and I help him up. "What's happening?"

"Invasion of the mind controlling bugs, Olympian. Welcome back to the right side."

"Who are ... I don't feel so ..." he doesn't finish, but manages to power puke all over my suit.

"That's it, get it all out and go guard Aphrodite. Make damn sure no one gets close to her! I've gotta go protect Andy."

• • •

Days later, the infirmary is full and the corridors are littered with the walking wounded suffering withdrawal from a drug they can't remember. Everyone has lost the last three months of their memories except for me, Stacy, Andydroid, and a few busted Cyber Dudes. We were even forced to zap Holly and Keisha after they were reinfected.

Stacy hasn't left that throne except to eat and go to the bathroom in two days. I stop by to see her, as often as I can. When she isn't speed dialing through the area codes and making international calls, she's broadcasting thoughts of happiness and peace to areas already cleansed of the vermin. I wouldn't want to pay the Olympic-sized phone bill they're going to have after this. They're supposed to be getting her some damn help any day now. She's been working her ass off for them as it is.

Naturally, being one of the few fully functional supers, I'm already on riot duty and putting out fires all over Washington DC and the surrounding area. Every few hours, I feel Stacy's empathic wave pass over and everyone is calm for a short time and then the shit starts up all over again. It's worse than any war zone imaginable.

By the end of the first week, I'm almost convinced that we should have just let the bugs win. If it wasn't for Stacy, I'd go back to my base and hide out until all this was over.

Landing, I go to pickup fresh powercells and start connecting them. There's a crowd out front, so I go in through the roof entrance. Andy nods to me and waves. Most of the other heroes are uneasy in my presence, unsure of what to make of me. The still convalescing Poseidon is especially wary after learning that his stint in the infirmary was at my hands.

"If it isn't my favorite dispatcher, how are things, Andy?"

The remarkably human-looking mechanical being hooked to the telecom board blinks several times, processing hundreds of phone calls. "It's not good out there, Cal, but you know that better than I do. They're mindwiping St. Louis, Kansas City, and the Dallas/Fort Worth area today, but we're still behind schedule. Entire cities are burning."

"Yeah, people figured out how to cut out the bug glands and extract the drug from them. Now they are fighting over the dead bugs as well. That's only made things worse. What's with the crowd?"

"The President is giving his first speech and trying to do what he can. Are you not supposed to be *en route* to the riots in Richmond?"

"Low on energy," I answer looking at the big screen and see the gaunt and tired face of our President. There's Stacy right next to him and next to her is ... Ultraweapon.

"My fellow Americans and citizens of the world, we are climbing out of the abyss. Every hour brings us closer to putting this dark time behind us. We are diligently working to get more the memory erasing units out to all the countries. One hundred units alone today left for Europe and another two hundred are heading to Asia. Three additional empaths are now on duty and our heroes are providing around the clock infusions of positive energy. Things will get better! These are surely our darkest days, but the light of hope is on the horizon."

I tune the stuffed shirt out. Considering my felon status, I couldn't have voted for him even if I wanted. Instead, I'm staring at how close Ultraweapon is standing to Stacy.

"... and I'd like to thank the people up here who were directly responsible for our salvation from science gone awry."

"What the hell?"

Everyone in the command center makes an effort to avoid looking in my direction.

"Screw it! I'm going out there!"

Zeus and Apollo stand up and move in my way. The lord of lightning says, "You're not going anywhere. You're supposed to be in Richmond anyway."

I flip my mini-gun around and spin the barrels making my intentions clear. Hermes shouts, "No one do anything! I'll be right back!"

From the corner of my eye, I spot Hermes speed into the screen and whisper into Athena's ear. They immediately exit stage left. The hothead and the lightning rod look ready to rumble and I'm quickly getting into a mood to oblige.

Andy's head swivels a full one hundred and eighty degrees and says, "May I request that this fight not occur so close to the fragile equipment of the communications center."

Crenshaw storms into the room and shouts, "Stringel! Stand down!"

"You're on thin ice, Crenshaw. Choose your words carefully."

"Look, be happy you're getting a pardon and a paycheck. You want someone to blame, I made the call."

"Why?"

"I see no reason to act like we're buddies. Here's the deal – the world is still recovering and it needs the reassurance that the heroes were looking out for them."

"Even if it's a lie?"

"Damn straight! They don't need to know that the only reason we're free is because some petty crook was too scared to get out of his armor and got lucky."

"So this is how the hero gig works. The guy who caused all this gets lauded for the greater good and the guy who fixed it gets a knife in the back!"

"Just hold up your end of the deal, Stringel. You'll get your money and a pardon. Then, you can get the hell out."

Somehow, her words fail to have a calming effect. The only thing that stops me from cutting loose is Stacy walking into the room with Ultraweapon.

Her eyes immediately light up. At least someone's happy to see me, "Cal! You're here! I thought you were in Richmond."

"That's where they wanted me."

Her gaze shifts between Athena and the armored warrior standing next to her. "I see we've been busy making backroom deals, while I've been stuck on that damn throne."

"Stacy, be reasonable..."

"What's this all about?" The Love Goddess cuts to the chase.

Ultraweapon points at me and says, "You're serious about this clown?"

"Yes. I realize that you're missing the last three months of memories, but I'm not. Here's the short version. We broke up. It was mostly your fault. I've moved on. Deal with it. The person I'm really disappointed in here is you, Holly. Seriously, what are you thinking?"

I put a few things together and my mouth starts working before I have the full picture.

"It's Patterson. He's not going to play nice with the rebuild unless he gets the girl. That's why I was sent on my merry way. You know what? I just thought of something, how long was it after you two broke up did billionaire boy and his wondersuit go after the Overlord's base? I'll bet my pardon that Patterson was trying to prove something to Aphrodite."

Suddenly, I feel like less of an obsessive dickweed. He's way out of my league when it comes to that. His mask hides his expression, but I know the truth.

Athena says, "It's nothing of the sort."

"Sure it isn't." I fire back.

Several things happen in the next instant. Stacy turns on Athena and they both start shouting. Ares steps in carrying a pallet of freshly constructed Mindwipers. He sets them down to rubberneck at the blossoming catfight and Ultraweapon grabs one. Time freezes as I shout for Stacy to look out, but I'm too slow.

The aura hits her and fades. Ares grabs Patterson's wrist, yanks the device out of it, and pins him to the wall.

Stacy looks all around. "What's going on? Why am I in this getup? Holy shit! What happened to my hair?"

Athena immediately rounds on Ultraweapon. "Patterson! What the hell did you do that for?"

From inside his high-tech mask, he cackles, "If I can't have her, I'm sure as hell not going to let some cheap knock-off have her! I never lose! Do you hear me?"

I barely hear him; I'm still staring at Aphrodite. She's not Stacy anymore, or at least *my Stacy*. I start forward, but Athena, Zeus, and Apollo jump on me to hold me back.

"Let me go!" In close quarters, all his gadgets are practically worthless. I've already learned that lesson.

Ultraweapon taunts me even though he's still firmly in the War God's grasp, "Sure let him go. The chump thinks he can take me."

Athena slaps her hand over my helmet force blaster. "Stringel, let it go! Stand down! Not in here, dammit! Ares, get that piece of shit out of my headquarters. Patterson, you get your slimy ass back to the west coast. You want to play power games with your company? We'll make sure the press gets wind of your involvement in this whole mess."

Patterson shakes off the Olympian's hold and addresses us. "You don't want to go there, Holly. There might be consequences. Enough! I'm going. I said, I'm going! Stringel, anytime you want to bring that sorry excuse for a suit out my way, I'll be happy to kick your ass, punk."

"You'll never see me coming, bastard." I hiss.

He walks away laughing. "In your dreams, knock-off."

They keep holding me until he's gone. Athena finally says, "We're going to let you go now. No funny business. No flying off the handle, if you still want that pardon. You get me?"

"I get you, but I want an explanation, bitch."

She starts to look angry, but then holds up her palms. "Okay, you deserve one. He begged me for another chance with her and we go back a ways."

"And you didn't approve of me."

She doesn't bother denying it, "That too, but I'd never have backed him if I knew he'd do that to Stacy."

"Do what to me? Why do I have the feeling I'm missing out on something?" Aphrodite asks and looks at the pallet of high tech weaponry. "What's with all the Mindwipers? Oh great! I just got wiped didn't I?"

Athena looks at her and then at me. "Stringel, go get something to eat in the break room. Someone else will cover Richmond. Andy, can you reroute WhirlWendy? I'll bring Stacy up to speed and then come get you. For what it's worth, I am sorry."

The bitter anger is replaced with an empty numbness. A few of them have the decency to look ashamed. I walk away with a simple, "Whatever."

• • •

I eat mechanically, not even bothering to appreciate the pun. Not to anyone's surprise, Ares, Zeus, Apollo, and Poseidon all seem to have decided to get something to eat at the same time. Isn't there a world in chaos out there? Holly might be "sorry," but she obviously doesn't trust me. I don't blame her.

Andy was nice enough to contact me via the dispatch system right as I entered the cafeteria. His message was one of simple encouragement, "Should you opt to disassociate yourself with the Olympians, I would be interested in a possible team-up in the future. You have proven to be a valuable ally and, given your current capabilities, I would be reluctant to face you as an enemy on the battlefield."

Andy is a stand-up kind of ... guy, so I told him I'd be interested as well. We're part of the ever-shrinking club that knows the whole story. Suddenly, that seems more important than ever.

Forty-five minutes pass and Aphrodite, not Athena, walks in. She dismisses the rest of the Olympians and approaches. "Hi. Mind if I sit down?"

"It's your base. I'm just … well I don't know what I'm doing."

She smiles saying, "They've got someone to do that thing with the chair for the next few hours, so I've got a little time. I hear we were an item?"

"Yeah."

"How long?"

"Only a few days."

"Really, but you were ready to go toe to toe with Ultraweapon over me? Must've been intense."

Unable to meet her eyes, I turn away and say, "It was for me."

"I believe you. You're not the kind of guy that I usually go for, but maybe that's the point. Holly says that you're responsible for my haircut."

Letting out a hollow laugh, I shrug and say, "While you were detoxing from these bugs, I kept you prisoner. You weren't terribly thrilled about it. I ended up putting a helmet on you to keep you from firing your psi-bolts. Unfortunately, your braids wouldn't fit. You salvaged it after you got clean, but were still kind of angry with me for a few weeks."

"I'll bet I was. I also heard that you're the reason the world got saved in the first place."

I shake my head, trying to look anywhere but at her. "Well, if you can call around-the-clock riots, looting, and civilization on the brink being saved. It's a mess out there."

"So, what do you want to do, Cal? Are you going to keep working to get your pardon, or are you going to hightail it out of here after we finish eating?"

"I promised you I'd hang around and try to make an honest go of it. You may not remember, but I do."

"Odds are, I probably will remember," she says and pats the hand I'd removed the gauntlet from.

"Come again?"

"I've been hit by a Mindwiper before. For someone who isn't a powerful psychic, the memories would be gone for good, but fortunately, I am a powerful psychic."

"What does that mean?" I ask getting my hopes up.

She wrinkles her nose and replies, "Last time, they started coming back first in my dreams … bits and pieces at first. Eventually, they reassembled themselves into memories."

"How long did it take?"

"A few months. It might take less this time, especially since I've been exposed to it before."

"You've got some footage in your armor's hard drive. That might help you remember sooner," I offer trying not to sound downtrodden.

"I saw that in my room. Your handiwork? I'd assumed it was Lazarus."

"You assumed a lot of things about him. Even if you don't remember anything about us, don't trust him. He's no good for you."

She opens her mouth and I expect to hear the Ultraweapon fangirl drivel she spouted when I first captured her. "From my recollection, we just broke up and I was pretty happy about it. It was getting to the point where I was just some kind of trophy to him. Plus, he just Mindwiped me. I'm unlikely to forget that anytime soon."

"Unless he does it again," I say.

"Nah, those things can't go back any further than three months and the brain creates a resistance to them that gives an immunity for the next year or so."

"Really?" I say, already trying to figure out how to make myself immune to it when I'm outside my armor. If I modify one to just whack a couple of hours, but still generate the immunity, that could work. I'd need to analyze the beams wavelength and frequency first and then see how it could be jammed.

"You still here, Mechani-Cal? You looked like you were drifting."

Hearing her call me that is just wrong. "Just thinking of a way to prevent that from happening to me. Just call me Cal, please. So, you want me to give you the rundown on how to work your armor?"

"Did I really want to keep it?"

"You were able to fight Athena and Hera to a standstill in it."

"Really?" she says with a gleam in her eye.

My helmet is sitting on the table. I flip the faceplate up, call up the archived video of the battle in Missouri, and turn it around so she can see. She watches with considerable interest and smiles at the end. "I'd never thought of getting my own set of armor. I guess I will need that refresher course."

I reach out with my one bare hand and cover hers. She hesitates, but doesn't pull away. "You told me once that you felt like one of the weaker Olympians. You're not. Don't ever sell yourself short, Stacy. I didn't really save the world. I just put the pieces in place so you could."

The heroine tilts her head and stares at me until I ask her, "What?"

"Outside of the Olympians, everyone always calls me Aphrodite, even Lazarus. You just called me Stacy."

"You'll probably remember why. It started because you were strung out and not behaving like a hero. I called you Aphrodite when you turned yourself around, but mostly in the field when we were on a mission. Around my hideout, you didn't seem to mind Stacy. Do you want me to call you Aphrodite?"

"No, it doesn't sound right coming from you, but that tells me how close we were."

"I hope that's a good thing," I say.

"It is," her tone is reassuring. "I have a small confession to make. Holly was going to come out here and let you down easy and send you down south. She told me that I shouldn't bother and that you were just in it for the money."

"Yeah, that sounds like her. So, why didn't she?"

"Andydroid interrupted with an emergency that required her presence. After she left, Andy admitted it was a ruse and showed me the video of us in the trophy room during the big battle and then right before I got zapped by Ultraweapon. I got a few things out of it."

"You did?" I ask and decide that my new best friend is Andydroid.

"Well, the first was I obviously wanted to be your girlfriend and the look on your face was priceless. I had a similar look on my face when I came back in from the President's speech. I was really happy to see you."

Swallowing hard, I say, "You're pretty observant. What was the other?"

"If you were only in it for the money, you wouldn't have run back outside and fought that berserk mob of heroes and villains … and by fighting, I mean you did some serious damage. I thought Holly, was just being silly when she told the others to come in here and make sure you didn't throw a super-tantrum, but after seeing that video and the one you just showed me of the two of us fighting together, I can see why."

"I guess I finally made it off the D-List," I joke, feeling a bit self-conscious.

She gives me an "oh please" look and continues, "Andy said that I was more confident around you and based on what I've seen so far, I believe him. I may not know the first thing about you, but I know you were important to me."

"I want to believe you," I say.

She shakes her head and replies, "My movies bombed. I was never that good of an actress."

"We actually joked about that and agreed that you weren't all that bad. Everyone stopped going when they figured out that you were never going to show any skin."

"Oh really?"

"Really. So, are you sure you want to keep me around? Other than Andy, you're not going to find too many people that approve."

"Yeah. It looks like I'm stuck here for the time being and you're out in the field, but I don't see why not. Besides, Holly meddles too damn much and she needs an Olympic-sized ass chewing. Remember in the video when I said you need to make more of an effort to get along with her? Well, she's going to get the same speech. As for the rest of the world, it's none of their damn business who I date!"

I'm stunned by the fierceness of her tone. No one has ever stuck up for me like that. Either she really is an incredible actress, or all this means something to her as well.

Seeing that I'm at a loss for words, she continues with a take charge tone to her voice, "So, here's the bottom line. You're going to stick around. We'll take it slow while I get my memories back. Then, we'll play it by ear and see what happens. Any problems with that?"

"None. Just get a recording of you putting Holly in her place. I'd pay to see that." We both share a laugh before I continue, "What about Patterson? He's one breakdown away from going over to the other side."

"Holly and the others are going to keep a close eye on him. I'm washing my hands of it and he needs to get over me. Either way, he's their problem and I'm going to use this to get him out of my life for good."

She's trading him for me? "Are you sure?" I'm trying not to get my hopes up, but it's hard. This seems too good to be true.

"Positive. I should have never let him become more than just a friend." She pauses. "Why do I suddenly have that song running around in my head?"

I can't help but laugh. "Just a friend, you say? That's our song."

"No, I don't think so. I never liked that song. If we do have a song, it's definitely not that one." Despite her protests, she's relaxing and enjoying herself. It's a good sign.

"It's probably the ray affecting your memory. You love the awesomeness that is Biz Markie."

As we sit there and engage in witty banter, I see where my life is headed, and for the first time I'm more hopeful than bitter. I always thought I was just one unlucky break from being the next Lazarus Patterson.

Well, screw him! He can keep his suit and the teams of engineers that built it. I like mine better. The money? I'll have enough. Who cares if the rest of the world doesn't know or even care that I'm the real hero? Stacy does and that's all I need.

Chapter Six

Riot Duty is Like Going Back to High School

Naturally, by the end of the next week, I'm already rethinking my decision and reconsidering a life of crime. Once again, I've found a way to go against the grain. Here I am, trying to get on the "straight and narrow," and everyone else has turned into a mass of strung out, petty criminals. Finally getting a paycheck is even more ironic because money doesn't seem to be worth anything right now.

Shaking my head at the foolishness of it all, I turn my attention to the problem in front of me. Riots have turned a good portion of Charlotte, North Carolina into something resembling a third world country and three guesses who they want to lend a hand?

On approach, I notice that what little had been left in the superstore from when the insects had taken over, has been looted and the folks left around are enjoying a good old fashioned four alarm fire. A ring of overturned vehicles blocks the two fire engines that are trying to get close to the Wal-Mart and a ragged line of a hundred or so cops and National Guardsmen are making a half-assed effort to drive off about five hundred shouting delinquents.

I'm somewhat torn. Drive them off and they'll simply reform elsewhere and burn some other place to the ground because it doesn't have any food inside. It almost makes me miss the bugs … almost. When the hive mind was in charge, trucks just dumped grain and other food at places where the "drones" were working and that was that.

Take away the mind controlling part and people weren't so inclined to put in a hard day's work and the infrastructure of the country collapses like a house of cards. The mass of sheep out there want to be able to go to the drive thru or have that pizza delivered. Unfortunately, gas is being hoarded. Fuel is being hoarded. Hell, I'm sure toilet paper is being hoarded and as a result hardly anything is making it into the major cities.

Anything that does usually is ambushed at the city limits by these "checkpoints" that are popping up.

To the survivalist whack jobs out there, this must seem like a wet dream come true. Then again, I have a secret base with a large freezer filled to the brim with frozen waffles, shelves stocked with toilet paper, and other things. So what exactly does that make me?

Hovering over the crowd, I toggle my external speakers and pull up an audio clip of the same spiel I'd given a hundred different mobs in a hundred different cities. "Please cease and desist. Return to your homes. Follow the instructions of your local authorities for the duration of the crisis."

That gets the "boos" going and my threat assessment software begins tracking all the projectiles incoming. Mostly it's just empty glass bottles and garbage, so I sit there and take it and let the pissed off mob expend a little energy.

I'm only carrying a twelve round magazine of tear gas grenades and the day just started. It's going to be a long one. Resisting the urge to just "gas and go," I catch one of the liquor bottles and toss it into the air. My helmet mounted force blaster tracks the target and I vaporize it just as the bottle reaches its apex.

I cut off the looping audio file and look back down at the crowd. "Alright! Now I have your attention, let's try this again. Go home. Do you really think burning down a Wally World is going to make things better? When they finally do get the food moving across the highways again, how does this help?"

Pointing at the cops and the guardsmen, I continue, "Maybe if you all weren't here, they'd be somewhere else fixing other problems around this city instead of wasting their time with you dipshits."

"Where's the damn food?" self-appointed bullhorn guy yells. "People are starving here!"

The bugs would have given old Charlie Darwin something to smile about. If figures were to be believed, world population was down about half a billion. Those that couldn't work were allowed to die off and did so with a smile on their faces. Those who were overweight got on an involuntary weight loss program. Statistically the world is now a much healthier, but not terribly happier place.

As evidenced by the crowd below.

I try the nice guy approach. Yeah, that's a bit unusual for me, but I'm open to suggestions. "Look. Things will get better. Keep rationing what you have and stop burning shit to the ground."

"When are they lifting Martial Law? What about our freedoms?"

"Do I look like a guy who knows when that's going to happen? No, I'm on my way to another riot in Columbia, South Carolina and got diverted to your little pep rally here. Maybe the governor will consider lifting martial law when you stop rioting? Ever think about that, genius?"

After a few more exchanges with the idiot with the bullhorn and the crowd completely agreeing with him, I had my fill of being a nice guy. A quick check on wind direction and speed and I fire a spread of tear gas grenades. Four quick thump thumps from the forty millimeter and I had a nice little cloud of gas spreading across the group of rioters.

I suppose settling an argument with tear gas is poor sportsmanship, but Athena and her ilk consider me a warm body, good for shit like this. That's not a very high bar to meet, and I'm not really trying to exceed their expectations. Besides, the way I look at it, I gave the guy a good five minutes of my time and now it's time to pay up.

Of course, picking up one of the overturned vehicles and threatening to throw it at the guy might have been excessive and I'll probably have to try and hack whatever footage might show up online, but the crowd is now officially scattering. As a former president might say, "Mission Accomplished!"

I stick around long enough to move the overturned cars and let the fire engines get in there before flying south of the city to Interstate 85. The one functioning police helicopter is reporting another one of those "toll booths" has cropped up. Entrepreneurs or modern day highwaymen – probably a bit of both, but since they have guns and are bent on terrorizing the people trying to get into the city that puts them in the way of what the current ringmaster at 1600 Pennsylvania Avenue is calling The Great Recovery.

From my perspective I'm going to get a clean start, a paycheck, and at least for the moment, I can rough up a few idiots without pissing anyone off that much. It's a win-win scenario. Most scatter when I land, but a young mother and her maybe eight-year old kid fire once at me and immediately drop their weapons. The kid's looks like a pellet pistol. They want to be arrested.

"What exactly are you two doing?"

"I heard there is food at the jail," the woman says. "You can leave me, but please take him."

"They're in as bad a shape as everywhere else. Sorry." I try not to look at their faces. "Just try and hang on." I hope they straighten the food transportation problem out soon. There haven't been any reports of cannibalism yet, but it is only a matter of time. The milk of human kindness is a bit curdled these days.

"Please, you must have something … anything."

"Mechanical? Are you still in Charlotte?" A female voice cuts in on the priority frequency. I don't recognize it and she doesn't get my name right.

"Hold on a sec," I say to the woman next to me and cut my external mike. "Yeah, I know I'm supposed to be halfway to Columbia, but there were some complications. Who is this anyway?"

"It's Wendy. No, I'm actually glad you're still in the area. I need backup over near the basketball arena. There are reports of a super in that area who is still infected with the bugs and causing problems."

Here I was expecting to get jumped on about being behind schedule. This is a pleasant surprise. WhirlWendy – the teenage tornado maker – well technically, she's out of her teens now, but that's beside the point. Since she ran with the New York City crowd and I mainly operated in the south, our paths didn't cross much and I don't really know her except from what I see in the media.

She's pretty, if a petite, Italian American, B-cup, brunette with a pixie cut is what you're looking for. I generally like women that are more substantial, but that's just me. Anyway, Wendy La Guardia - a distant relation to the guy they named the airport after - has been in the superhero and acting gigs since she was a preteen, and that makes her an "old hand" at twenty-one. Her mother runs Wendy's vast merchandising empire and her father is the senior Senator from New York and chairs the Senate Superpowers Oversight Committee. As one of the most popular heroes in the world with all kinds of powerful friends and family, it's a bad idea to make an enemy out of her.

"Any idea who it is?"

"No, that's why I called in for backup and Andydroid said you were nearby and on this frequency."

"Okay, I'll head over that way in a couple of minutes. Let me finish up here."

"Understood. See you in a few."

I look back through my visor at the hungry mother and her kid. Yeah, I'm kind of a lowlife with no qualms about tear gassing a crowd over being on the losing side of an argument, even if I was right. Turning on my external mike, I send the command to pop my side access panel and march her back to a battered SUV where she's out of everyone's line of sight.

"Look! I'm sick and tired of people asking me for food. I don't care. I don't have any either. I'm not going to arrest you either, so you'll just have to take care of yourself and your kid. Do you understand?"

At the same time that I'm reading her the riot act. I point toward the open panel and make an unscrewing gesture with my gauntleted fingers. She gets the hint and reaches inside and unhooks the food tube and slides the item into her large, but mostly empty purse. It's got two pounds of chicken dumpling paste inside. Not exactly scrumptious, but if I just gave it to her, any thug watching would confiscate it and possibly kill her. Maybe I'm getting soft, but I push it off as I'm not that hungry right now.

Besides, I like the beef stew better anyway. Yeah, that's it.

• • •

My onboard sensors start acting funny as I close on Wendy's position. She's darting around in the air and it looks like something is chasing her. All the interference is making it hard to lock on. I magnify and see some humanoid shapes leaping at her.

Swiveling my six barrel pulse mini-gun around, I accelerate. Without solid targeting information, I have to eyeball it and make certain to avoid hitting WhirlWendy. My first burst knocks a couple backwards, but doesn't seem to cause any injury. That's not supposed to happen.

The first one I can get a clean look at appears to be some kind of phantom punk princess with her hair in a Mohawk, along with spiked wristbands, and dog collar. She's flying at me with no visible form of propulsion and I see no point in trying to talk to them. Wendy is probably much better at that and they attacked her anyway. I zap her with my helmet mounted force blaster. She takes it right in the kisser and goes flying back about twenty feet ... but that's it!

A second one, this time it's a nerdish looking youth with an equally phantom laptop in his hands rams into my side and checks me like we're in a hockey game. Whatever they are, they're solid. I throw an elbow and brush him off.

"I thought you were going to wait for me?" I yell at Wendy.

"I thought I was too! We've got to get through these and down to him before it's too late!" She points down at the ground.

"Who is that?" I ask while fending off a jock in a letterman's jacket with a baseball bat.

"I think its Imaginary Larry," she replies scattering three others attacking her with a gale force wind. "These things are telekinetic constructs."

I'd heard of this guy, but never thought I'd run into him. He's not really a hero or a villain, just a force of nature with multiple personality disorder. The onset of his massive powers screwed with the kid's mind. He's been going to his imaginary high school inside his mind for a little over the last two decades. All these constructs we're fighting are his pretend schoolmates, the stereotypes and clichés of every drama and sitcom imaginable.

"Any idea how to stop him?"

Wendy says, "The Olympians wore him down by beating these things until he passed out from the exertion, but that took hours and they had the whole team."

I dig around in my mind for an idea. Reinforcements aren't anywhere around. Actually come to think of it, they're just a phone call away. "I'll keep his friends busy. Try to get outside the range of all this interference and have whoever's in chair saturate this area. Maybe they can stop him."

"Alright," she says and rockets upwards a thousand feet. I drop down to the ground and fire my remaining tear gas grenades at the real person. My plasma mini-gun spits out energy, but what must be Larry's glee club appears to shield him, while the cloud of gas starts to envelope him.

They're singing a pretty good cover of the Bee Gee's *Staying Alive* interrupted by the barking of the mini-gun. Larry starts coughing and his constructs imitate him, but the cloud is dissipated by a wall of force that knocks my suit back twenty feet and I land in a heap. His burst knocked my shields down to sixty percent and he wasn't even really aiming at me.

Yeah, I didn't think it was going to be that easy either. Finally, I get a good look at Larry. He's got at least four bugs on him! Maybe he'll burn out even faster. I crank up my cannon and augment it with my force blaster. Larry counters with sending his school's marching band into my burst. The glee club switches to *Oh When the Saints Come Marching In.* I feel like the universe is screwing with me.

Something smashes into my back. I spin and find the track team. It was the shot putter and it hurt. My jetpack is damaged … can't risk going airborne.

Dodge the discus. Watch out for the javelin. Keep an eye on the mini-gun's energy levels … half depleted.

I try to cut through to the source of the problem, but he keeps generating a never ending wall of constructs in front of him. If they were real, I'd have mowed down an entire graduating class at this point. They just keep coming! Can't seem to make any headway either.

Where the hell is Wendy? I could use some effin' help here.

Thirty seconds later, my main weapon is out of juice and I'm left with just the blaster in the helmet and my force field encased sledgehammer. That's not good. On some level, Larry senses it too. The Glee club starts a rendition of Hammer's *U Can't Touch This*.

As if on cue, the sky darkens. Swinging away, I can't follow WhirlWendy's progress. They're swarming me under. The sledge is knocked away from my suit's hands. With a high voltage burst, I blow them off of me at the cost of more of the armor's diminishing power supply.

There's a momentary opening, and I make use of it. Scooping up the sledgehammer, I smash through the concrete wall of the arena and get inside. For a minute, I wonder if Larry out there can just make new constructs without a line of sight. Maybe he could if he was sane, but he's not and that's the point. The Mechani-Cal sized hole I left limits the number that can attack me to a manageable number.

Plus with a busted jetpack, I don't want to be sucked up into the air by Wendy's assault. Believe me when I say that long, hard falls aren't really much fun and should be avoided whenever possible.

The constructs continue fighting, but with a little breathing room, I can see Wendy at the end of the street. She's hovering, eight stories up, in the middle of a growing funnel cloud, and looking to bring the pain. Part of me is jealous; Larry and Wendy can tap into a ridiculous amount of power with hardly any effort. Me? I have to spend hours working on the suit, hours charging powercells, and even more hours repairing the suit after a short fight.

I remember a couple of years ago, they had one of those specials on cable where they took Wendy down into the Texas and Oklahoma area and let her slug it out against Mother Nature in Tornado Alley. It was all one big publicity stunt to promote her first action/adventure/romance movie – *Blow Me Away*. Not surprisingly, after she saved a few trailer parks and used a counter vortex to sap the strength out of a nasty looking F3 that had Tulsa in its crosshairs, her movie did rather well. The engineering geek in me actually calculated how much energy that stunt required.

Yeah, things like that really impressed the girls. Then again, I'm now dating the sexiest woman on the planet, so who is laughing now? Assuming I live through this mess, can fix my jetpack, make a token appearance down in Columbia, and make it back to Mount Olympus, Virginia by eight tonight, I'm supposed to have my first public outing as Stacy's newest boyfriend. That seems unlikely at the moment.

Knocking a Goth girl and a cafeteria lunch lady back through the wall widens the gap and now, three of them can get through. The howl of the wind picks up announcing Wendy's approach. Her maelstrom tosses most of the constructs aside like toy soldiers. Some scatter, but many of them just disappear. My attention focuses on Larry, who is beginning to glow with a bright light as he senses the threat.

It's going to get ugly fast, but the real question in this super powered game of chicken is who is going to blink first. Wendy has set herself up as the unstoppable force and – despite my best efforts – Larry is still one helluva immovable object.

Brushing off a group of slow moving attackers, I lumber down the corridor toward the main entrance as veritable rain storm of broken glass showers me. The two titanic forces collide right as I reach the broken windows and start through them. I get thrown right back inside by the backlash and bounce off a support column. It's a struggle to get upright. Master alarm. Shields are down. My hammer is missing. I'll find it later! Main power is at forty percent and either my heads up display has double vision or I do. The armor is going to need some serious down time. For that matter, I probably will as well.

The next thing I notice is the synth-muscle damage in the left leg makes me stumble like an armored wino. The good news is, I don't have to look very hard for a hole to get back outside. There are several options to choose from. I pick the one with the least amount of debris and work my way out into the dust cloud outside.

Making best speed, I head for the center of the cloud. When it begins clearing, I see the two of them. At first I think Wendy pulled it off because she's hovering off the ground. But then I realize that Larry has both hands around her neck and is holding her up like a rag doll. Her legs are kicking and flailing.

Shit! He's choking her. Shit! Shit! Shit!

The force blaster on my helmet still works, but the targeting system is out. My sonic screamer is more likely to hurt WhirlWendy than it is Larry. It looks like going mano on mano – or is that mano on psycho – is my only choice. I try to build up a head of steam and do my best to stay pointed at him.

He spots me when I'm about fifteen feet away and more of his telekinetic constructs start to form. I dive onto the ground and trigger my damaged jetpack. The thrust propels me forward as I smash through the constructs and take Imaginary Larry out at the knees. Wendy gets thrown clear and it's just the two of us.

Okay, I've got him now what?

I'm so close that I can see the four bugs attached to his neck. Rearing back I try a punch with my right hand, but his powers just leave it hanging in the air. There's that damn Master Alarm again. I really do need to change it to something less obnoxious. I turn on the sonic generator and let him share my audible discomfort. That's not working either. Hands from his constructs are trying to pull me off. I've got one hand still wrapped around his waist.

What the hell? Why not? Mass release on the way. *Charging!*

My left hand pulses with high voltage electrical power and I turn into a giant defibrillator or bug zapper – take your pick. The first jolt makes him arch and release a gusher of energy. I get thrown clear. The sonic generator cut out and so did the Master Alarm. No readings on the power meter. I can still move, so I crawl back to him. He's still glowing and it looks like the bugs survived. I smack my right hand down on his chest and vent whatever I have left in the suit. The second eruption is every bit as violent as the first and is compounded by the new damage to my armor. Exposed synth-muscle must've caught some of the burst as my suit does its best impression of an epileptic seizure.

There's absolutely nothing left for a third jolt. Hell, I can't even move. I can see Larry's limp form out of the side of my faceplate. He's not moving either. At the moment, it's a draw. Wendy steps into view and she kneels down over Larry, checking on his condition. A couple of systems are coming online. Neural commands aren't working. The backup verbal ones are. It takes three attempts, but the faceplate finally opens and I get a few gulps of fresh air … well not exactly fresh air. It's more like ozone and burnt hair.

"Is he alive?" I ask.

"Still breathing," Wendy responds in a raspy voice. "The bugs are toast. Nice move there. Thanks for the assist. How are you?"

"Good question. I think I'm okay. I'm not having problems breathing and it doesn't feel like I'm bleeding anywhere. That said I feel like I got my ass kicked a dozen times over and I'm betting my armor looks like hell."

She laughs and makes a painful face. "If you can still gripe about it, you're probably okay. Darn it! I thought I had him with that twister. Hey, what are you mumbling about over there?"

"My neural gear is still down. I have to make do with voice commands. If I can bypass enough damage, I should be able to move again."

"Do you need me to help you out of the armor?"

"Maybe. Give me a few minutes to see what I get running. Are you calling for backup? If the forty year old high school senior wakes up, I'm going to have to sit this round out."

"I've already done it, Mechanical. Apollo is bringing his chariot."

"See if he'll bring some powercells and my spare jetpack."

"No problem," she replies.

"By the way, whatever happened to getting help from the person in the chair?"

Whatever I just said, it seems to have struck a nerve. Wendy looks angry enough to kill … well probably not that. She is a hero after all, but she does look pissed off enough to really hurt somebody or give them a talking to.

"The ass hat in the chair was MindOver," she answers. Wow, she actually said a bad word. She must be ticked off.

I'd search my database for info on whoever this guy is, but there's a small problem of all my systems being down. "Okay," I admit. "What does that mean?"

"He told me he was too busy and we needed to handle it on our own."

"Remind me to kick his ass, sometime. Any idea why he would leave us high and dry like that?"

Wendy looks like she's searching for the right words. Finally she says, "He's an empath, who used to stalk me a few years back and kept using his powers on me, despite the fact he was in his late twenties and I was sixteen. My parents figured out what he was doing and got him booted out of the East Coast Guardians and sent to the Northern Frontier Guardians in Montreal. They must be scraping the bottom of the dumpster if they're letting him get in the chair."

I've got movement in my right hand. That's a good sign. Hopefully, I can walk this suit out of here under its own power. Dignity counts for something. Still, I'm interested in Wendy's story. The superhero "community" goes to great lengths to keep little stories like this from getting out despite the efforts of the tabloids and the paparazzi. Back in my gun running days … ahem, armament innovation days, I'd catch a snippet or two that did get out – a little gossip amongst supervillains. It was always just enough to make me wonder what was really going on. Now, I realize that behind the rose garden is a big old pile of fertilizer stinking up the place.

"So I take it you're not his favorite person," I say.

"I used to be until the restraining order," she answers and points to her necklace. "My father had Promethia make some psionic dampers for me to wear to block his powers."

Arching an eyebrow, I say, "Really. Any chance I could get my hand on one of those? I'm looking for ways to protect me from Mindwipers when I'm not in my armor and wouldn't mind picking up some extra protection against telepaths and empaths."

She considers my request. "Normally, I wouldn't. No offense, but I don't know you from dirt. But after what Ultraweapon did to Aphrodite, I can't really feel any pity for him or his company. He's almost as big a creep as Matthew Mather."

"MindOver Mather?" That's stupid, really stupid.

She nods and continues, "Supposedly, he's descended from the guy that did the Salem Witch Trials."

"And everyone keeps telling me my name is hokey."

The little brunette laughs and some of her New York accent slips through. "Hello? This is WhirlWendy you're talking to here. The name sounded good when I was like twelve. We were looking to change it right before the whole bug thing happened, but the focus groups weren't big on either of our two options."

"Focus groups? You've got to be shitting me! I'm beginning to think I should stick to being a villain."

"Fraid so," she says probably noticing the scowl on my face. "If you're going to stick around on this side, you'll probably want to get an image consultant as well as an agent."

I scowl some more.

"Look at it this way, Mechanical. The money from the appearances and the licensing will help make repairing your suit easier."

The squirt has a point. I can't exactly start knocking over jewelry stores when my spare parts supply runs out.

"Thanks," I say, trying to sound grateful. "I'll keep it in mind for later and hit you up for the details then."

"Okay, I'll introduce you to my mom sometime. She handles all the details. I just show up where she tells me and sign what she says needs signing."

For a moment, I consider saying how I couldn't trust anyone – not even Mom and Dad – with my money, but I know that's one of the differences between me and all these "goody two shoes" that I'm surrounded by. It is interesting to get some insight from somebody who isn't an Olympian.

One leg is working now along with one arm. I can at least crawl now. Wendy is quiet for a few minutes while I keep fiddling with my onboard systems. The area is blissfully free of rubberneckers, since Larry had driven most off earlier and then my partner there busted out a tornado. I'm sure eventually some will show up.

"Hey," Wendy says. "There's a good chance that I might be taking over the Gulf Coast Guardians when they reform. Athena said you've been assigned to the pool of new Guardians candidates and that you used to operate out of that area. You interested?"

"I guess so. What do you guys do? Have a draft or something?" I wonder if there's a signing bonus.

"The four team leaders are supposed to be meeting next week to fill the gaps. Except for She-Dozer and José Six-Pack the roster is gutted and I'd be starting over from scratch."

Wow! That *is* stripped bare. "José is the groundskeeper! I mean his power is just making five clones of himself. They're gonna let him go on missions? Why do you even want that job?"

She shrugs and spreads her hands. "I'm never going to be a leader up in New York. I keep losing the vote for deputy, too. They still see me as a kid. It's time for a change of scenery."

"So if that's the case, why are they letting you take over one of the Guardian franchises?"

"Money. I've got more than enough to bankroll my own team. I almost quit the East Coast team after the last deputy vote, but I stayed after they promised I could transfer if a leadership position opened up in one of the other teams. When no one else looked eager to take the Gulf Coast job, I said I'd take it. Bolt Action tried to block me and keep me in New York, but I reminded him about that little promise of his. This is their way of letting me go off and still keeping me in the organization. The team has image consultants too and it would've looked bad with one of their most popular heroes leaving."

"Louisiana is going to mangle that accent of yours," I say getting the suit up to one knee. Hurray for progress. "You sure you want me?"

"Well, you did pretty good today and Aphrodite speaks highly of you. Your recent combat footage isn't shabby either. The East Coast isn't interested and the West Coast ..."

I finish for her, "Is a bunch of Ultraweapon ass kissers."

"... not exactly the way I was going to put it, but sure why not. So, you've got New Orleans or Montreal to choose from. How do you feel about the Frozen North?"

"Who else are you trying to get?" José is a scrub and Sheila Dozier is okay for a strong girl, but she can't fly and isn't that much stronger than the suit I'm wearing. Anytime I fought the GCGs, I just stayed in the air and used my force blasters. The most She-Dozier could do is toss stuff at me, but her being a hero, she was reluctant to damage people's personal property. If I'm going to be part of a team, I don't want to be the only one besides Wendy that can handle an emergency.

"Chain Charmer is available, but I heard the Northerners are after him. I think I have the inside track though. Andydroid is tied up for the next two months with the Olympians until they get their new switchboard computer, but he said he might be forming a duo with someone else, so I'm not sure. There's a few of Doc Mangler's experiments and a couple from your side of town out there looking for a fresh start under the second chance program."

"Andy is waiting on me," I say. "If you take me on, I can talk him into coming when he's finished being the Mount Olympus phone sex operator. I've heard Chain Charmer is pretty good. Did he and the Grey Logger break up?" They kept trying to go by a different team name, but "Link and Logs" stuck and eventually the same sex partners accepted it.

"Grey Logger went down fighting the bugs. He was one of the first to die. The information was in the computers at Mount Olympus. Now that he's been wiped, Chain Charmer is still trying to come to grips with it. He's leaving Seattle."

"Sorry to hear that," I say and gesture to Imaginary Larry. "Too bad you can't recruit a powerhouse like him." I get the armor to a standing position and make my first wobbly step – so far so good. The power meter shows nine percent. If Larry does wake up in a fighting mood, I might be able to give him a couple of shots with my force blaster and then spit on him. That's about it. A couple of determined Eagle scouts armed with can openers could take me in my current condition.

Looking at the older man in the burnt letterman's jacket, I see his hand twitch. "Um, Wendy. Sleeping beauty just got his kiss. What do you want to do?"

She grimaces and pulls off her mask. "Alright Mechanical, I've spent a third of my life in teenaged sitcoms and dramas. Just follow my lead."

• • •

"So let me get this straight," Stacy says, looking at the mangled mess that is my armor spread out on two workbenches. She's changed out of that heavenly strapless number she'd been wearing when my sorry ass arrived into some jeans and an oversized tee shirt. Good God! She could make a burlap sack look appealing. "You show up three hours late for our date and you're idea of spending time with me is for us to work on your armor? That's not exactly sweeping me off my feet. You could've at least bought flowers."

Thankfully, her tone is teasing. Andy told me that she was one of the people ripping MindOver a new one for letting just two supers take on Imaginary Larry. Maybe his new name should be BendOver.

"Hey," I answer eloquently. "I had a lot on my hands tonight. I was never good at basketball and there I was as the new basketball coach for Larry's high school against their arch rivals for the State Championship. It was so intense."

We're in one of the underground warehouses below the Olympians base. It's like one big techno junk pile. The Olympians employ a cleanup team that follows behind them and removes all the debris from their battlefields. Whatever can be reused or recycled or is just too damn dangerous is sorted out. The rest ends up here. Yet another thing that I'll have to get used to – picking up after myself. Villains don't generally worry if they leave depleted uranium shell casings all over the place, or cadmium residue, and so on. Most of it is too battered to be of any use, but I'm down here scavenging synth-muscle and anything else that might come in handy. I like this place. It's quiet and reminds me of my old junkyard hideout.

"I'll bet," she laughs and hooks up an arm to a diagnostic computer and then makes a face saying, "Eew. This needs a full rewire. So what role did Wendy play? Cheerleader?"

I poke my head out from inside the chest piece. "No, she was my trouble making younger sister, who just transferred to the school. I told Larry to keep his eyes off of her and on the game. She said it was like every cheesy after school special she'd ever been in rolled up into one big ball."

"Go on."

"Well, I got the lights on in the arena and we sat there with a bunch of Larry's fake people and I coached the game of my life. You should have heard my halftime speech. I'd have recorded it, but my audio mikes are shot."

"I suppose Larry's team won."

"Time was running out and we were down by two with just fifteen tics on the clock left. Our best shooter had turned his ankle, so I told Larry it was all on his shoulders. Fortunately, Apollo was waiting outside and I had Larry shoot the three pointer to win it, because winners don't play for no stinking overtime!"

My date is amused. "Of course they don't. So what happened next? He made the shot?"

"From almost half court. It was nothing but net! I'm pretty sure he was fouled too, but the idiot refs weren't calling anything all night. Anyway, I shook his hand and Wendy gave him a peck on the cheek as all his telekinetic constructs carried him on their shoulders around the arena." I pause and point to my heart. "It got me … right there."

"I'd call bullshit, but it sounds like you managed to have a good time."

"Except for all the damage to my armor. Still, I might just have to go back to his facility … err high school for football season."

Stacy chuckles and says, "I do love a happy ending. Wendy probably didn't like it. I heard the last two seasons of her show she was trying to get out of her contract without doing anything serious to mess up her squeaky clean image that she fools everyone with."

Wendy has a wild side? "What? No sex tape? Nothing says, 'Get me out of a contract,' like a good video romp plastered all over the internet."

Stacy rolls her eyes. "Why are guys so obsessed with sex tapes? You won't ever catch me in one. It's all just so … what's with that look on your face, Cal?"

"Um," I stall for time and try to think of the best way to break this to my amnesia burdened girlfriend. "You might want to rethink that statement."

She gets an incredulous look on her face. "Seriously? You're not pulling my leg? No, really? How the hell did you ever talk me into something like that?"

"Actually, it was your idea," I answer looking for somewhere I might hide. This wasn't exactly first date material. My plan was to let her remember it on her own or tell her sometime, anytime as opposed to right now. "In fairness, you were … uh … well you were worried about the bugs getting you again and it was the night before we were attacking this base. You might have been feeling a little impulsive and reckless."

She crosses her arms and is clearly not amused. "Where is it?"

"At my base. In a safe, on an encrypted USB drive and not connected in any way to the internet. I don't even keep a copy on my suit."

I wouldn't put it past Ultraweapon or someone on his payroll to try breaking into my suit's computer. I'd like to think I could catch someone doing that, but I'm just one really smart guy. There's only so much I can do. That said it feels like the temperature just dropped about twenty degrees in here.

"Just see that it stays there," she says. Her expression becomes unreadable and I feel a twinge of guilt. I have to cut her some slack. We've only kissed a couple of times since she lost her memory. I'm honestly beginning to wonder if she's just marking time with me while she tries to figure out what she saw in me in the first place. Hopefully, she starts recovering those memories soon.

"Well, this is awkward," I admit after a pause. "How about we change the subject? Wendy wants me to join the Gulf Coast Guardians when they reform. She said you had a hand in her offer. Thanks."

She relaxes a bit and smiles. "Don't mention it. Holly put in a good word for you also."

"I'd thank her too, but I think her motivations are less about me being on a team and more about me being over a thousand miles away."

"Be nice," she cautions.

"That was me being nice to her," I respond.

"So, are you going to take it?" Stacy asks.

I set the chest plate down on the bench and nod. "I'd hoped to be closer to you and maybe get a shot on the East Coast team, but it sounds like New Orleans or Montreal are my only two options and since it's about the same distance from either of those two places to you, I'd rather be warm – thank you very much. Until then, I guess I need to get my suit fixed, so I can get back out in the field on riot and food convoy escort duty. It'd be easier if I had minions."

"Minions?"

"Well yeah," I answer. "Nobody messes with Hades and those shadow monsters he makes. Imaginary Larry had an entire high school worth of lackeys."

"Too bad all those Type A robots we had in Missouri were destroyed."

"Yeah, they're in a scrap yard somewhere. Then again Type A robots are honestly more trouble than they're worth, unless you're using them to guard something. Anything else and I'd be spending all my time fixing them on top of fixing my suit. Now if I had a Type B or two that might work. They're tougher, easier to maintain, and mount a better array of weapons."

She points over my shoulder. "There's bound to be something you can use in those piles. You want me to look around back there?"

"Actually with your strength, I know you can wind synth-muscle bundles tighter than I ever could. If you want to do that, I'll poke around and see if there's anything other than a bunch of broken stuff."

Stacy agrees and I head into the junk pile, armed with a flashlight. Part of me is eager to find something cool, but a larger part is worried that we are already drifting apart, and I'm not sure I can fix that. At my base, she developed so much confidence in her abilities and herself. Now, she's taken a few steps backward and seems hesitant. Being unsure of herself, it doesn't take a genius to see that she's just keeping me around until she decides whether I'm worth her time.

Relationships aren't really my strong suit. Like that's a big surprise to anyone. When it comes down to it, I'm not even sure that *I* like Calvin Matthew Stringel that much, but I'm playing the hand I've been dealt, and I'll go as far as it will take me.

From the sounds of things, I'll be on a team full of superheroes soon. I'm already cringing at the thought. How's a selfish, out for himself, bastard like me going to rub shoulders with a bunch of do-gooders without going insane?

Those are today's million dollar questions and, like always, I'm a bit short on cash.

Chapter Seven

Further Proof I'm an Asshole

Taking a deep breath, I look at Stacy. She isn't bothered in the least. It's pretty silly for someone who's faced the dangers that I have, but I'm nervous anyway. I feel naked and nervous without my armor.

"It's not too late to slip out and go watch a movie. We can say hello to all the nice photographers that have been tracking us like bloodhounds," I say hoping she agrees.

"Oh, it won't be that bad. C'mon, I'll prove it," she says opening the door. "Mom, Dad. We're here."

Great. Just flippin' great. It's meet the parents night. To make matters worse, mine are here too. I hadn't seen them since shortly after I got out of prison and that went over so very well. A few months later, there were arrest warrants out for me, which made visits for the holidays somewhat difficult – not that I was interested in trying.

People come into the foyer to meet us. Dad looks like he's lost weight along with a bunch of hair and Mom looks smaller than I remember. The fact that she's using one of those four-legged canes sends a pang of either guilt or remorse down into the pit of my stomach to disturb the butterflies currently there.

Dad is beaming. I get a man hug, complete with a slap on the back. "Good to see you, son," he says.

"Nice to see you, too. Hello Mom." I lean down and give her a hug and a kiss on the cheek. Neither is really returned.

Me being a supervillain kind of put a negative spin on Mom's active social life. The poor life choices I'd made impacted her standing in her gardening club, church, and just about everywhere else she went in my hometown. I didn't encourage her to brag to everyone about my getting a full ride to UCLA or the job at Promethia. She's was the one playing the "my son is better than your children" game with all the other women on her block. Suffice to say, there's a bit of a grudge being held there. Being a supervillain means you never have to say you're sorry, unless it's to the judge or the parole board. Even then, it's only an option. Odds are it won't change what's going to happen.

Dad, after I was tossed into the slammer, never had any expectations. Apparently, I've exceeded his wildest dreams lately. The guys at the lodge and down at the bowling alley Dad manages are probably getting an earful now about how his boy is dating Aphrodite.

Stacy's parents are giving me a critical once over. Doctor Harrison Mitchell is tall, slender man who is a renowned physicist and author who usually spends half the year lecturing all across the world. I'm an electrical engineer, not necessarily in his league, but I can follow what he says. Then again, I might be out of touch when it comes to the latest views on superstrings, but I can build a powersuit. Can he?

His wife is a lawyer and a lobbyist for green energy and definitely not your usual socialite and trophy wife. The father might have the brains, but the mother is the one with the killer instinct. I greet her with a polite handshake and the same with her father.

The niceties last until just after I finish my dinner salad when Ophelia Mitchell asks, "So young man, I'd like to know why you turned to a life of crime."

"Dear," her husband says, "Can your cross examination wait until dessert?"

I clear my throat. "Bad decisions, Ma'am. There's a long version, but in the interests of keeping it simple, it ultimately it comes down to a series of bad choices on my part."

"Well that leads to an interesting question. Does one good deed outweigh the sum total of one's bad decisions? What do you think, Harrison?"

"If life were an equation, so easily solved by balancing the good and the bad, the solution would have been reached a long time ago, dear."

It doesn't seem like her husband is taking her bait. Suddenly, I'm liking the man more and more.

"I'm just happy to see that Calvin's making something of himself," Dad chips in. "Never thought my boy would make the top ten list on *The Late Show!*"

Considering the topic was *Things People Can't Remember About the Bug Invasion* and a picture of me was shown with the caption of, "Proof that being one of the last available men on the planet can actually work!"

The guy with the big chin on the other network wasn't nearly as harsh. Here I thought people who get their fifteen minutes of fame are supposed to be able to enjoy the ride.

"Yes, but it's only a matter of time before he messes this up as well," Mom contributes. Absolutely no bitterness there. My luck with the females in this room is limited to Stacy and we're just doing "okay" at the moment.

I feel the heat on my face, but I work through it and just keep eating. Looking at Mr. Mitchell, I ask, "So what was Stacy like as a child?"

"Very happy and mischievous," he answers. "She had a way of doing things that made it impossible to stay upset with her. I just wish Hannah and Nikolai were able to be here this evening."

Somehow I doubted Stacy's siblings would help the already charged atmosphere, but as an only child, I couldn't be sure.

Dad tries to get a thought in. "Calvin here was a real pistol, always taking things apart so he could see how they worked. I used to go to yard sales just to buy broken electronics so he'd stay away from the vacuum cleaner and the VCR."

"So you're saying he had a pattern of disregarding other people's possessions?" Ophelia comments.

"Mother," Stacy says in an emotionless tone. "Your disapproval is duly noted, but this is dinner and not an inquisition."

I force a smile and offer, "If you've got an inkblot test, I'd be happy to take it after dinner. It would probably be more fun than Pictionary."

If she actually took me up on it, I'd have to tell her that the first card looks like her daughter's vagina. That would go over well.

"Are you trying to be clever, Mr. Stringel? If so, you're failing."

"Wouldn't dream of it, Ma'am. I'm just trying to get through the night without any major incidents. Nothing I can do or say tonight will change your opinion of me. I'm something of an acquired taste. My decisions were bad, but if you're looking for me to apologize for them," I pause for effect before concluding, "you're sadly mistaken."

"I see," she says, conceding. "Perhaps we should discuss something else. I've heard Promethia is moving forward with their combined solar and wind initiative in California and they're going to absorb the costs of any budget overruns. Yet another instance of generosity from Lazarus."

I give her credit. She does go for the throat. "I'm sure the profits from his military robotics division will offset any potential loss for the shareholders of his company."

Of course, I could counter her argument by saying that Ultraweapon's one "bad" decision caused the bug invasion and in addition to all the blood on his hands by virtue of his military hardware that he's also at least partially responsible for roughly a half a billion dead people worldwide. But, it's all good because some tree huggers are happy! What do I know?

The rest of the meal continues on the same theme. Mrs. Mitchell looks for avenues to needle me while her husband does his level best to recuse himself from the festivities. Mom joins in at odd intervals to emphasize how she can't trust me anymore after I've made her bitter. Dad eventually surrenders and stops trying to offer anything helpful about me. He's outmatched by this crowd and stabs at his entrée and dessert with disinterest. For her part, Stacy stands by me, but I'm not certain whether it is for me or to spite her mom. I do my best to keep things civil, but I'm almost glad the two mothers came with their mental pitchforks. I don't mind people being angry or disappointed by me. It's when people are being too damn nice that I get uncomfortable.

Good times. I just love 'em. I should have gone on a riot patrol instead. At least then, I would have been able to knock a few heads around or tear gas a group of people just because I can.

• • •

Riding the hoversled back to Mount Olympus, Stacy says, "I'd expected my mom to be on her worst behavior. I'm sorry that turned out so badly. Our dates don't seem to be going all that well so far."

"There was no bloodshed, so it wasn't that bad," I say dismissing the evening. "I'm guessing you didn't enjoy yourself."

"Not really," she answers. "Did you?"

"It was a date with you. I'm not complaining."

"That's sweet," Stacy says. I don't tell her that I've had that line ready for the past eight hours. I didn't need any kind of precognition to know how the evening was going to turn out.

"Thanks. Your parents weren't going to like me. You've got a pretty good idea what mine think of me. Now we have an excuse for not doing that again for at least six months. How about our next date we just take a boat out on the Chesapeake Bay and get away from the photographers, the parents, the other superheroes, and everything else? Do you like to fish?"

With her driving, I can't see her face, but she says, "No, but I like relaxing in the sun. It's funny. I almost didn't go on that cruise in the Mediterranean. My parents were supposed to take me to Australia instead."

I hadn't heard this story before. "What happened?"

"Some legislation was put on hold in a committee in Congress. Mom cancelled to go do her lobby thing and Dad didn't want to go without her. So, I managed to get on that yacht at the last minute. Sometimes, I wonder what would have happened if I didn't make it. Would they have still taken me from wherever I was or would somebody else be Aphrodite? What about you, Cal? Suppose Promethia never came after you with that no compete clause. Would you have been happy at Ubertex?"

"I used to think I would, but now I'm not so sure. I was an arrogant sonnuvabitch. I'd have probably stayed there a year and looked for the next big raise. Either way, it didn't happen. That's for the best. Otherwise the bugs might not have gotten stopped. I don't have any regrets. You in a hurry to get back?"

"Not particularly. My shift in the chair doesn't start for another four or five hours. If I'm late, Mather can just deal with it."

I don't have an issue with her sticking it to that rat bastard. "Why don't you land on one of the rooftops? We'll just hang out and watch the stars."

"Last time I did that, a group of Rigellians landed."

"Were they trying to take over the planet?"

"No, just bounty hunters looking for Gravmatar."

"Wrong continent."

"I didn't say they were good bounty hunters," she responds and laughs while landing on an apartment building.

Looking out over the DC suburbs, I get my hopes up that something can be salvaged out of this train wreck of a night. For thirty seconds, it seems like it just might happen. Then, the wind shifts direction.

Stacy coughs a little and my eyes tear up. The stench is overwhelming. She finishes and says, "I hope they start picking up the trash soon."

"Yeah, that'd be a nice start. I'm guessing the Gulf Coast is in even worse shape."

"Did we ever go to a junkyard?" Stacy asks out of the blue.

"That was my first base. It was destroyed. Are you getting some memories back?"

"Just a flash. Maybe it was the smell that reminded me of it. Was it a dive?"

I get over the unintended insult and admit, "Actually it was better than my other base."

• • •

One month later, after a quick stop by my secret lair – I upgraded it since I'm supposed to be "one of them" now and hideouts are for criminals – to pick up some supplies, I'm passing the outskirts of New Orleans and in sight of the Gulf Coast Guardians' headquarters. Last time I was here, I didn't have time for sightseeing. I was just here to steal … liberate their jet and lead the attack on DC.

I think I've said it before, but I always looked down on the GCGs. Some of the solo heroes down this way command more respect. It was the last of the Guardian franchises to be established and it shows. The fact that this team was essentially mothballed during the crisis with just a couple of heroes left to lend a hand while everyone else was pulled to the East and West Coast teams probably won't be forgotten anytime soon by the region.

But now, we're "reopening." I'm sure they're waiting with open arms. Open palms is probably more like it.

WhirlWendy wants to turn it all around and show everyone that she can be a leader. Good luck to her. I don't intend to mail in my performance, but I'm not jumping for joy and looking to make an impact just yet.

The mansion is a converted high school that was shuttered in the late seventies, used by the National Guard as an armory in the mid eighties and occupied by the Gulf Coast team in the late nineties. Warm and friendly are not words used to describe this place. The chain link fence topped with barbed wire is knocked down in places and still hasn't been put back up. Several windows look like they were busted out, probably by looters. My sensor array spots four Type A's walking inside the perimeter. Yeah, like those will stop anyone!

Frankly, I'm in a bad mood. My relationship with Stacy is stuck in neutral. Other than the occasional flash of a memory, she still hasn't been able to reconnect the dots. My date on the bay ended up being spoiled by cloudy skies and some industrious photographers in a rented helicopter, who were tipped off by the place we rented the boat from. Stacy wasn't impressed when I started suiting up to chase them off. The picture of me flipping them off looked nice on the three heavily trafficked websites that bought it.

"Cleared for landing on the helipad. Boss lady wants everyone in the briefing room," José, or one of his clones informs me. He sounds bored. I can't say I blame him.

The only good thing about the response to this crisis is that it's making everyone forget how badly everyone flubbed it during Katrina. The bugs relocated most of the populace, which was why I liked it during the early days of the invasion. Obviously, the bugs didn't want to build in places that were technically below sea level. Maybe they were onto something.

The helipad is on the roof of the main building. Both helicopters are missing. I look over at the airstrip that was built where the football field once might have been. The main hanger is still half-collapsed from my last visit here and the fight with the few active robots that tried to prevent our little grand theft airliner. The place needs some work. Hopefully, Wendy will let me put in some gun emplacements and replace those tired ass Type A robots with some less tired ass Type B robots that I might be able to locate if there are any left in those other bunkers that used to belong to the Evil Overlord.

I leave my belongings in the cargo elevator and walk toward the conference room. "Time to make nice and play well with others," I say to no one in particular.

The door opens and I feel like it's the first day of school. The table is rectangular with a view of the digital map of New Orleans and the surrounding area on the plasma screen.

"Mechanical," Wendy greets me. "I'm glad you're here. We're already up to our necks in problems. You and I are the only two heroes that fly. The Navy has one of their USNS ships coming in this morning. They can't pull pier side. There is nowhere to put them even without the rioters. Their helicopters are down with engine problems. Until they're back online and the pier situation is under control, we're going to need you to unload it and fly the pallets into the warehouse. José prime and two of his clones will hold down the fort and the rest of the team will be there to provide security at the distribution center."

I look around and see casual indifference from Chain Charmer. His main weapons are six magical chains of various lengths wrapped around his body. Occasionally they rustle and the ends rise, giving the appearance that they are alive. He uses them like extensions of his arms and can use them to propel himself around and encircle his enemies. Charmer is shorter than me, with jet black hair and no shave anytime in recent history. With his normally boyish Asian looks, he now reminds me of a bad guy in one of those cheap martial arts movies. He's skinnier than I'd seen in pictures on the internet and looking kind of gaunt. There's little doubt this is due to the death of his spouse, Grey Logger. Their wedding was televised on one of the cable channels.

I still have my faceplate closed and nod to him. Seated to his left is Dozier. Sheila is a big, intimidating Amazonian at least six foot six and the only hero to return from the previous lineup. It's probably just as well. I didn't have nearly the level of interaction with her as I did with some of the others. The bags under her eyes make me wonder when the last time the blonde got any sleep.

Five of the six José's are in the room. The other one must be on monitor duty. That's got to be depressing! Does he get six votes or just one when we have to decide on something?

Between a pair of clones is Anemone, a Manglermal created in Doc Mangler's lab. Old Doc had himself a super soldier program funded through DARPA turning volunteers into hybrids with increased strength, speed, and other benefits. I wouldn't have minded giving it a whirl, but it turned out that there was a sixty percent mortality rate among the volunteers and the reversal process never did quite reach the production phase. The Doctor was able to successfully bury those minor details for a brief time, but eventually he lost his big fat Uncle Sam contract and was forced to go into hiding. The Improved Humans Program was phased out and replaced with the automated soldier project headed up by Promethia and other competitors.

It didn't stop Mangler. If anything, his bottom line improved once he hit the black market. The criminal underworld didn't really care as much about their foot soldiers. It was one of those "can't make an omelet without breaking a few eggs" things.

Anemone's dark skin secretes a powerful paralytic and, according to Wendy, was one of the few that the bugs couldn't get at because of that fact. Supposedly, the Jamaican gangbanger hid out on a derelict oil platform off the coast of Mexico until the threat was eliminated.

He wears a protective suit that collects his juice and allows him to spray it in a pressurized mist or stream. The downside is that his dates have to wear these full body condom things or get off on being paralyzed. From what I understand, it's not pretty. The upside is that he's a natural – if that's the right word – at crowd control! He's working off three grand larceny convictions and numerous lesser offenses – criminals of the world unite!

The other Manglermal is a lizard lady who calls herself, Kimodo. She must be a new convert because she doesn't have a criminal history or she has been smart enough not to get caught. My guess is that the lady is strong, a leaper and does a good job climbing sheer surfaces. As I examine her, she flicks her tongue at me.

The last face gives me pause. No, not him! Please God no! Despite my fervent wishing, there he is … The Biloxi Bugler. He just grins at me and gives me a wink. Of course he had to come out of retirement. The first stinking hero I ever lost to … the guy who sent me to prison … I have to work with him?

"Are you okay with that, Mechanical? If not, we can switch and you can help get all the freighters and tankers free that are aground on the banks of the Mississippi. You're probably better suited for carrying cargo since my winds would probably damage the pallets and such and my wind won't punch through the hull of a ship like you would." Wendy asks and I realize I haven't said anything yet. It's probably unnerving her.

"Yeah, it's cool. I'd rather be a cargo hauler than a tugboat. It doesn't matter to me. I just need to change out my powercells and pack some spares. We're in for a long day." Somehow, my first day on a super team doesn't look so epic.

"Okay, until we can get some sense of normality around here, I'm not going to hold a deputy vote. Sheila is well known in these parts and she's going to be the deputy leader for the foreseeable future. If anything happens, I won't be more than a half hour away. Any questions? None? Good then Onward Guardians!"

I cringe as Sheila, the José's, and The Bugler repeat it with gusto. Chain Charmer mumbles it while I look at the two Manglermals and try to remember why I signed up for this in the first place.

• • •

"I'm glad to see you finally on the side of the righteous, Mechani-CAL. You've come a long way since ManaCALes," The Bugler corners me back at the cargo elevator and says. At least he's putting the right emphasis on my names. He at least respects me enough to do that or he's anal retentive. It could be both.

"It seemed like the thing to do at the time Bugler," I answer. "I didn't even know you were on the squad. You look like you've dropped a ton."

It's true. He's in as good a shape as when we first fought all those many years ago. In his retirement speech, he admitted that he had adult onset type two diabetes and that it was time for a younger generation to answer the clarion call of justice or some similar garbage. It's another case of the bug diet plan getting some people healthy while others were just made to die.

"It was strange. One day I'm watching strange news on the television and digging the costume out of the closet. The next thing I know, I wake up and I'm one hundred and ten pounds lighter! As for why I'm back, I have to believe I was spared for a reason. Just like you, Mr. Stringel, I've been given another opportunity and I know I still have something to offer."

"Why did you want to join a team this time? You had a pretty good solo gig going."

"I'm just a reservist, who has been activated until Andydroid is able to join us."

There's a light at the end of this tunnel! "Shouldn't you be getting to the sleds?" All this bonding is making me uncomfortable. I might have to hurl.

"It's a fresh start for both of us, Mechani-Cal. I want to put our past behind us and be good teammates. Feel free to call me Bo when we're not in uniform."

The bile is creeping up in the back of my throat, but it's a nice gesture, so I'll reply in kind. "Well in that case, I'm sorry I put you in the hospital that time. Speaking of that, you ought to think about wearing some thicker armor."

"My wife is making me look into it. That is part of the reason I asked to join the Guardians. She doesn't want me out in the thick of things by myself anymore."

"Sounds like she really cares for you," I say, still feeling uncomfortable. I have enough problems with my own relationship issues.

"That she does, boyo. That she does. So, what do you have there?" He gestures at the case I'm opening. Inside is one of the things I created out of the salvage pile at Mount Olympus.

"My second minion. It's a hover drone." I remove the three foot wide flying saucer object and lift it up for the hero to inspect. "I'm still working the kinks out."

"What's it do?"

"Right now, Floater can fly and responds to basic commands from my neural net. I've got room for a camera and a small modular weapon mount, but it has to be lightweight. I'm down to three options; a pair of micromissles, a compact pulse pistol, or a sonic oscillator similar to the one in your bugle."

The Bugler looks at the space available with a critical eye. "I'm partial to sonics, as you're well aware, but the mount is too close to your camera equipment. You won't be able to fire a sustained burst without damaging your camera unless you can move the mount or redesign the oscillator. If you'd like some help with it, I can assist. I think you'll have the same problem with the pulse pistol. My recommendation is the pair of missiles."

I often forget that many of these heroes are inventors in their own right. The Bugler's specialty is audio engineering. It'll be strange collaborating with him, since much of the sonic design I have been using is lifted from his own work.

"Sure, I guess so."

"If that's your second minion, I have to ask what your first minion is."

"Roller was too big to bring with me. I'm having it brought back from DC when the Olympians return this base's jet. I built it off of parts from six different Type B robots. It's bigger, stronger, and faster."

• • •

The main deck of the navy supply ship is a beehive of activity. If I had some free time, I'd offer to try and fix either of their choppers and get myself out of this monotonous job. Unfortunately, I don't have the luxury as pallet after pallet is waiting for me. There's a sling assembly that allows me to carry two at a time. When I first landed, the deck crew wanted me to pose for pictures with them.

I'll admit it is kind of surreal. I guess I'm famous now as Aphrodite's boyfriend. People actually want to be seen with me.

When they assure me the sling is reconnected, I grip it and check to make certain everyone is clear of the blast zone and activate the jet pack. It's a struggle to get up into the air as I turn back toward the city and the five mile trip to the warehouses.

They didn't want to use the warehouses near the piers because of all the protesters, rioters, or whatever they're being called these days are. Naturally, the ones in the know found out where the food was going ahead of time and are there. From below, I see them streaming like a line of ants. Actually, they're a little bigger since I'm not flying that high, so maybe they're more like lemmings.

Here I am congratulating myself for my rapier sharp wit and I almost miss the change in the crowd. At first, it looks like the rioters had finally reached the boiling point, but a whole bunch of them are running into the people making their way to the warehouses. It's a stampede of fools running scared. There was a time in my past where I inspired that kind of "run for your life or you're gonna die" fear.

I switch over to the feed from Floater, who I left outside the warehouse. Something is jamming it. I only get an intermittent fuzzy picture, but I can see a big hole blown in the side. The distant piercing sounds emanating from the Bugler's weapon reaches my audio receivers and confirms my diagnosis.

Ladies and gentlemen, we have ourselves some supervillains in the area. I drop my load on the nearest roof and raise Wendy on our emergency frequency.

"Wendy, Cal here. Something's going down at the warehouse. I think the team is under attack. Is anyone else on the line?"

There's a pause before Wendy says, "Negative Cal. It's just us. Better get there in a hurry. I'm fifteen minutes out."

"I'll be there in one minute. I'll try to let you know what's going on, but you might lose me as well to whatever is jamming their signal. I'm going in hot."

"Copy that, Mechanical. Good hunting."

Seconds later, the link to Wendy is drowned with static. Whatever or whoever is the source of the jamming is playing havoc with my systems. It gets worse as I approach and I'm forced to fly closer to the ground, in case my navigation systems go haywire. Besides, if they've been watching me come and go through the roof access that's where they be expecting me to come in.

Frankly, I'm just not that dumb. Circling around the back, I see a gaping hole where the wall used to be. I think I'll go in that way. Unfortunately, being on delivery boy duty has left my suit woefully under gunned. I don't have my sledge hammer or my mini-gun, so I'll have to focus on speed and just hit hard with what little I do have.

Strafing through the opening, I see rats … thousands of rats, crawling everywhere. That means that useless idiot Rodentia is here. There he is commanding his furry horde and firing a submachine gun like the psychotic little runt he is. Right next to him is the bloated form Gunk spewing that same sticky phlegm that's still all over the holding cells in my base. That crap hardens to a consistency of concrete when it dries. I couldn't even power wash it off. I should have done the world a favor and killed at least one of them when they were my prisoners, preferably Gunk.

Sending a shot from my force blaster at the two minor league clowns, I start looking for the ringleader of this circus. Kimodo and She-Dozer are down already. The rest have fallen back and are using the pallets for cover.

Wham!

Something knocks me to the ground and sends me careening into stacks of dry goods. Killing my jetpack, I try to get traction and slow myself down before I go right out through the wall. With that accomplished, I look around for who bushwhacked me.

E.M. Pulsive! I hadn't seen Eddie in a long time. He's a guy who can turn his body into electrical energy and we have a history together. I did some rent-a-thug work for him back in the day and he's going to be a tough nut to crack, because he's been known to give even Ultraweapon a problem.

Truth be told, one of the reasons I worked for "Empy" was I'd been hoping to team up and take a shot at Lazarus Patterson, but it never came to fruition.

"Good help is hard to find there, Empy? You're scraping the bottom of the barrel with these two."

"Ah, Stringel the sellout," he answers in that irritating buzzing drone he has when transformed. "Is Aphrodite as good a lay as they say?"

"Does that nympho whack job you call a girlfriend still use you to power her vibrator after you can't get it up?"

His response is a beach ball sized crackling ball of energy that vaporizes the pallet next to me. Nine millimeter shells from Rodentia's gun ping off my shielding and armor. It's distracting.

"Easy there, Empmeister or word is going to get out that you have a premature discharge problem," I mock him and fire the blaster in my helmet. It's been a long time since I could talk trash to someone. Bug controlled morons were no fun and upset, hungry rioters are too pathetic. There's a liberating feeling about insulting someone right before I take it to him.

"Keep running that mouth! You ain't never going to be anything more than just a chump in a tin can, *Calvin.*"

"That might be true Eddie, but my suit's waterproof," I answer and smash my gauntleted hands into the fire alarm. "Sucks to be you!"

The Cheshire cat grin on my face fades when nothing happens. Eddie tilts his glowing head. "Seriously? You're trying the old spray him with water and short him out weak sauce. No one told me that it was rookie day. The rats already chewed through the wiring and the line coming into the building is full of gunk."

I have to give him props for coming prepared. "It was worth a try. Say what you want about me selling out, but you're the one knocking over a food bank."

"I gotta eat too," he replies. "Besides, this is more valuable than gold right now."

I consider the options. When Wendy shows up, she can suck up a few thousand gallons out of the gulf and give him the monsoon treatment, but that will ruin much of the food in here. "How much will it take for you and the idiots to just walk away?"

"Huh?"

I point to the pallets destroyed around me. "We fight and all the food gets wrecked. You don't eat, the folks that were outside don't eat, and everyone loses. Why don't we make a deal instead?"

I'm certain the rest of my "team" just gasped, but I'm being practical here.

"Sure Cal, you take your little kiddie club and leave, while we clean out this place."

"Don't get so greedy? Take five pallets and get the hell out of here."

"Five pallets won't feed the rats. You're just worried I'm going to mess up that pretty little suit of yours."

"Fine, eight pallets is the final offer. Otherwise we fight, most of the food is destroyed and even if you win, you still get out of here with right around what I'm offering."

He gives me a high voltage smile and I think he's going to go for it. "So, you're saying I can walk with eight pallets and not pounding you into the ground or I get the same thing if I do rough you up. Guess which one I'm going to choose, Tin Man? You two," he says to his minions, "dispose of the others while I take care of him."

It seems like bolts of energy come flying from every direction. I dodge a few; take more than I'd like on the shields, and return fire as best I can. The pallet I scooped up to toss at him explodes in my hands in a gooey cloud of canned vegetables and peanut butter. I charge him knowing that it's going to hurt, but realizing that I need to do this while I still have usable shielding to protect me.

A glance to the side shows Chain Charmer has all his lengths of links in a defensive formation in front of the other Guardians. They snap like striking snakes at the horde of rodents attacking them, while Anemone's paralytic mist stops most of them cold. The Bugler's blasts push the piles of moving and unmoving rodents backward. A pair of José clones, lashing out with stun batons, protect the third clone who is tending to my injured teammates.

Eddie and I collide. I activate the power absorbers in my gauntlets to stop E.M. Pulsive from swatting me away and start draining him. It's the same thing I did to Zeus during the bug invasion – except Zeus was unconscious at the time.

I stick to him like a tick and he isn't pleased. "That ain't gonna work either. I'll just short out your systems in less than a minute."

The jetpack roars and drags us out the hole in the roof. "Maybe, maybe not. This suit is tougher than my last one. I guess we'll see if I can make it to the Gulf before you do."

Since he made sure the water won't come to him, I have to bring him to the water.

"No you won't!" Eddie thrashes and flares with power. There's my master alarm again. I should just leave the damn thing on. I've got the throttle on the jetpack wide open. We're not exactly on the straightest path back to the Gulf, but we'll make it.

"You'll drown when your suit shorts out!"

"Buoyancy. I'm already pressurizing the suit. Don't worry about me Eddie, but if you land face down and pass out you're going to be the one that drowns. I'm not the one ready to die over some food."

"Screw it! Ten pallets. I'll take the damn deal," he shouts.

I slow the jetpack, grateful that I didn't have to find out whether my suit would actually float or not. "It's about damn time you came to your senses, Eddie. Truce?"

"Yeah, yeah, truce," he concedes and stops assaulting my systems. In response, I stop trying to drain his energy. "You're a real bastard, you know that?"

"It's my calling," I answer. "What are you doing back down this way? I thought you were working out of St. Louis."

"Damn bug brained people converted my base into one of those stupid factories. Hell, I probably helped."

"The bugs got you too?"

"Yeah, your effin' girlfriend. I ran into a bunch of the Olympians who were slugging it out with the Silicon Sisterhood. Zeus wasn't there, so I just hung out and enjoyed the show. Aphrodite spotted me and attacked. I shot back."

"Let me guess … She said your blast killed her bug. You brought her back to your hideout where she propositioned you?"

"That sounds about right. How'd you know? I turned back into my human form and she cold cocked me. Next thing I know, I'm a happy, happy, joy, joy drone lovin' me some bug smack."

He doesn't sound like all the other strung out bug victims. "What happened?"

"I can't stay in either of my forms all the time. Eventually my body changes and it got rid of that garbage in my system when it did."

"You didn't have to detox?"

"Not really," he explains. "I'm different like this."

We come back through the opening in the roof. Not much has changed, Gunk and Anemone essentially took each other out. Rodentia is cowering behind canned goods while controlling his furry army.

"Truce!" I bellow over the external microphones. "They're leaving with ten pallets of food."

Chain Charmer sneers at me and says, "You're just giving up?"

"Look around," I gesture. "Half the food in here is ruined. There's twice as much still on that ship out there. Let's quit screwing around and get the food to the people."

The rest of the Guardians don't like it, but that's their problem. I radio Wendy and tell her what's going on. She's not happy either. In the interests of getting on with my busy day in food delivery, I help put the pallets in the stolen tractor trailer and toss the paralyzed Gunk in the back with them. Ten minutes later, they and all the rats are gone and I get back to hauling food pallets and ignore the cold stares of the heroes.

Back at headquarters, both Wendy and the heavily bandaged She-Dozer corner me. Wendy goes first. "This doesn't look good, Stringel. The rest of the team thinks you sold them out. Jin checked the database and it said you used to work for Pulsive."

"So?" I answer looking up from the diagnostics I'm running. Fortunately, I only have a couple of minor repairs to make.

Sheila gets right in my face and says, "We don't make deals with criminals."

"We weren't exactly winning, but you wouldn't know that because you were on your ass."

"Cal, Sheila, enough," Wendy interrupts. "It just looks bad. Our first day out and we get walked over by a middleweight and two chumps."

"Would you like day two to go better?" I ask.

Wendy raises her eye and says, "What do you have in mind?"

"Well, I might have attached my floater drone to the underside of their semi. I put it in silent mode for five hours to make sure it wasn't detected while it recorded everywhere it went. It just uploaded everything a little while ago. So as soon as we go over the data, we'll know where Eddie's hideout is. I contacted the Olympians and Zeus is already on his way. Eddie is scared of Zeus because he can immobilize Pulsive with a wave of his hand. That's why Pulsive avoids the East Coast like a plague. Now, if you two ladies don't mind, I really need to fix my armor in case there's a fight tomorrow."

"Exactly when were you going to tell us all this, Mechanical?" Sheila practically spits out the question.

"First off, it's Mechani-Cal or just Cal if that's too hard. 'Hey you' even works in a pinch. I was going to tell you when I had a location. As soon as I finish this, I'll get it for you. Repairs will go much faster without you two bothering me, unless there is anything else."

Sheila backs off and Wendy looks like she ate something that didn't agree with her. Finally the team leader says, "That's fairly underhanded, Cal. We don't usually operate like that and I don't want it to become a habit."

"Duly noted, Miss La Guardia."

"C'mon Sheila, let's get you back to the infirmary. Cal has work to do and we should let him do it. José does the maintenance on our robots. I'll have him send in one of his clones to help you. Consider it an apology for us rushing to judgment about you."

She-Dozer mutters something under her breath and follows Wendy out the door. I can already tell that Wendy wants to be a "good" leader, but she placates too much. That'll lead to some problems down the road, but I'll worry about that bridge when I have to cross or burn it.

Eddie's big mistake was not taking my first offer. As much as I slam on these do-gooders, villains have their own set of problems. They're greedy, selfish, short-sighted (even some of the ones bent on world domination), and petty. On a level battlefield with the rest of my gear, I had a decent chance going up against Eddie. The problem is level battlefields don't really exist. Someone is always at a disadvantage. The secret is to make sure it's not you. Paranoia, it's not just a mental problem. It's also a defense mechanism.

• • •

The good news is my worrying isn't an issue this time. Pulsive's hideout is a plantation about twenty miles away with no gun emplacements or missile launchers. Eddie's crazy ass girlfriend opens the door and sees me in my armor with Zeus standing next to me. Her jaw drops.

"Um Sweetheart," she says. "It's for you."

"What?" he says coming out of the living room. "No! No! You suck, Stringel! Asshole! You two faced son of a bitch!"

"Sorry to say this, Eddie, but I'll put it in internet terms you can understand – all your base are belong to us."

I've been waiting a long time to use that meme on someone.

Chapter Eight

Emotional Purgatory

"Cal," Wendy says, entering the monitor room where I'm on duty. "Why do I have a 'Thank You' from the Governor of Florida and a request for two hundred additional robots?"

"It's probably just spam. You should ignore it."

"Don't give me that! What the hell are you up to?"

She obviously didn't buy that explanation. "Remember last week when José and I took the weekend off? Well we just happened to stumble onto a cache of robots that were just sitting around, not being used. Since all but five of them were Type A bots and not useful for anything other than basic guard duty, Andy and I reprogrammed them and leased the bots to the state of Florida."

Wendy slaps her forehead with the palm of her hand and says, "You stole somebody's robots and are leasing them to Florida?"

"Considering they were probably stolen to begin with, I prefer the term recycled. As for the agreement with the Governor, yeah it seemed like a good deal. Florida's in our jurisdiction, but even with our jet it takes a few hours to get out that way, so I figured this was a win-win for everybody concerned. We've got a hundred and fifty in a pilot program in Tallahassee and Panama City and I'm trying to round up some more bots. By the way, any problems with me taking tomorrow off?"

"Oh dear god! I can't believe you just asked that. Why are you doing this to me?"

"Doing what to you?"

"This! Undermining my authority. You could have done this on your own, but you obviously tied the Gulf Coast Guardians to your little money making scheme and that means me! What if someone takes over those robots and they go on a killing spree? You're a damn PR nightmare!"

"We've got it covered, boss lady. There are homemade 'R' shutdown daughterboards installed that either José, Andy, or I can access from anywhere. The operating system is "read only" and hardened by me first and then Andy. When they reboot, whatever coding someone tried to load is wiped out. If they've got an exploit that Andy hasn't accounted for, they probably deserve them."

"I'm still not comfortable with this. This sounds risky."

Doing my best to reassure her, I say, "We test them randomly each week. The paperwork is between my startup company and the state of Florida. José and Andy have spots on the board of directors; do you want one on it as well? It'd be honorary unless you're seriously interested."

Perhaps I'm having a bit too much fun at her expense. Technically, she is already listed on the board. Wendy looks ready to explode, so I adopt a more serious tone. "Look, I'm trying to make a serious go of this. I still don't have a pardon yet. Florida wanted these security bots, but wasn't going to do business with a convicted felon. Andy is an AI with no rights, and José has six green cards, so I didn't go out of my way to hide my Guardian affiliation. My armor takes a beating. Repairs cost money. That 'El Cheapo' stuff I'm building for José to augment his clones costs money too. My salary barely covers any of it and shockingly enough, Promethia won't sell me synth-muscle or any other parts directly, so I have to go through middlemen and pay their mark up. It's not fun."

"Can't you just do parties and concerts and collect appearance fees like Sheila, Bo, or Jin?"

I roll my eyes and respond, "Didn't you say, just last week that the less I interacted with the public, the better?"

"You leveled a YMCA in Pascagoula and then laughed it up with the local newscaster until the containment and cleanup team showed up."

"Technically it was Seawall. I just threw him there. He's the one that ripped those two load bearing columns out and tried to crush me. Hopefully, he signs up for those basic civil engineering courses at the SuperMax in North Dakota. I wrote the syllabus for it and they actually let me teach it during my time there."

"I think I hate you," she says and proceeds to begin swearing up a storm. I thought Miss Squeaky Clean didn't do that, but she hides it really well unless she's in private or maybe the pressures of leadership are already getting to her after just six weeks.

"It must be my special gift. Maybe that's why Charmer's spare necklace didn't work on me."

I'm kind of miffed. Charmer and the Grey Logger found some kind of rock either from space, enchanted by Indian shamans, or something while they were out looking for the next area of forest to clear and made necklaces out of it. I confess I lost interest in the tale about halfway through. Long story short, it gives normal people a super power. That caught my interest. I tried it on after The Bugler, who sprouted a pair of bat wings and elongated ears. It even screwed with his sight creating a sonar effect.

Me? Nothing that I could tell. I tried telekinesis, psycho kinesis, telepathy, levitation, and every mental trick I could think of. Hell, I even farted … well that just kind of happened, but I figured I'd see what might occur.

Supposedly, if a hero with a power tries it on, it weakens their power. Half of Jose's clones disappeared when he gave it a whirl. Now, I'm not sure if I have some kind of hidden power. I didn't feel any weaker. I could still think of all the things I needed to do with my armor - like anyone would ever accuse me of having super smarts.

• • •

"Nice to see you're settling in," Stacy says. Other than Dad driving down from home and a couple of state lawyers from Florida with contracts, this is my first real visitor. She's definitely the prettiest.

"In my own special way," I answer and smile. "It's nice to see they let you out for a change. Ready to party and let off some steam?"

"Well, it's Mardi Gras and the city wants to thank me for … I dunno …saving the world. My boyfriend being down here happens to be an added bonus."

"Probably good for public relations too," I add. "I get to be your bodyguard on the float."

"Any threats out there that I should be aware of?"

"Nothing in particular, but I'm sure some jerk out there is planning something."

"Might that jerk be named Lazarus?"

"I wouldn't put it past him. Ready to get showered by beads? I've rigged the float with an explosives detector and a force field generator that you can activate with this." I toss her a nice looking tennis bracelet that's been lingering around my base. "I'll have one activator and you'll have the other. It's the right there in the middle."

"You got this for me," she says inspecting it.

"Sure, let's go with that."

"Relic from the good old days then?" She swirls the ice cubes in her rum and coke.

"That hurts," I say and thump my chest. "Right here."

"It's probably just gas," she replies. "You should take something for that."

She's lucky I don't have super flatulence. I'd drop one on her in a heartbeat. "One of the nice things about getting a regular check is that I can afford a nice dinner as long as you don't come down every week."

Stacy tilts her head and sighs. "If it wasn't for the city's invite, I'd still be up in DC. They've built an augmenter that allows some of the less powerful heroes to stay on it longer."

"When are they going to start weaning the public off of the chair?"

"It's gotten political. It's an election year and the poll numbers are down."

I snort. "That's a shocker. Quick, let me put on my surprised face."

"I know."

"Any other interesting news?"

I listen to her gossip with interest. From Lazarus with a new model or actress on his arm every week, to the battle that just happened in Philly, the various holdups on my pardon, and Hestia hitting it off with that Mather idiot.

Eventually, I interrupt. "So, how about we go and get some dinner?"

"I actually think I'd rather stay in and raid the fridge. Where is everyone tonight?"

"Wendy's back in New York City for the weekend. All of José is south of the border visiting family. Andy's on monitor duty, Chain Charmer and The Bugler are on patrol, Sheila's dating or at one of her personal appearance, and Kimodo is out scaring babies or whatever she does. Anemone is filter feeding. What? Okay, he's at a jazz club."

"So we're all alone except for Andy?"

"Yup, this whole rundown base is ours for the taking."

She downs the rest of her drink. "Well in that case, let's go take a dip in the hot tub. I want to relax and unwind."

I did not expect that, but it's a nice surprise. "Sure."

"Lead on, MacDuff," she says misquoting the classics.

"The guest room is down the hall and third door on the left."

"You have a hot tub in the guest room. I misjudged this place."

"No, but I figured you'd want to change."

"Didn't you say we're alone?"

My secret super power must be creating lumps in my throat because one just appeared. She's being very forward. I'm pretty sure I like it. "Yeah."

"Then who needs suits? They just get in the way. Don't you agree?"

• • •

Later on, I'm on the thinking throne, doing my business and reflecting on what just happened. Stacy went back to her room and the bed seems emptier. Holly Crenshaw's cruel words from back at my base come to mind and taunt me. She once told Stacy to just jump my bones and cheer me up. From a clinical standpoint, I think that's what she just did. Don't get me wrong, I was into it and having a great time, but she didn't even come close to her "second level thing." I thought of asking her about it, but I was too chickenshit. The answer would've disappointed me. It's bad enough not knowing if she was faking it.

Call me crazy, but last night felt like an audition, and I'm not sure I passed. No, I'm not insecure. I'm way too paranoid for that. As long as I don't screw something up, things should be okay.

• • •

"Was that really necessary? You scared the hell out of those people!" Stacy is upset. I might have been a little quick to turn on the shield. I'm sure I'll hear about it from Wendy when she gets back as well.

"The explosives detector went off," I answer knowing how badly I just screwed up.

"Show me a set of beads that aren't covered in a layer of alcohol? It's Mardi Gras for crying out loud! Or it was until you came along."

The sound of the ambulances carrying the folks who were trampled fade. The shield knocked about twenty people back into the crowd and things got ugly from there.

"With all the laser pointers painting me, my threat assessment suite was going haywire."

"Then you should program it to recognize the difference between a laser pointer and missile lock. Ever think of that, Einstein? Shouldn't you have also told me that our float was really your oversized ball robot? When it came out with weapons hot, that didn't help things either."

"Would it help if I said that I'm sorry?"

"No. Just go back to your headquarters. I need to find a camera and try to salvage this."

"Alright. I'll see you later."

"Just go!"

A few hours later, a limo pulls up to the headquarters and I have all the all the tools of a proper apology ready. Unfortunately, it's just a driver here to collect her baggage and meet her at the airport. So much for her staying a couple of days.

• • •

"She's through with me, Andy. The Olympian's press manager won't even forward my calls to her." I'm crying in my cups to an android. He mans the monitor console and doesn't judge me. It's probably why I like him so much.

"The variables are too complex for me to give you a definitive answer, Calvin. That said, the indicators point toward a dissolution of your relationship. Would you like some possible course of action?"

I pop the top to my third beer and say, "Why the heck not?"

"Very well, I suggest a strategy with multiple layers. You should start by composing a poem, song, haiku or limerick. There is a high probability of success if that is your initial offering."

That's what I get for asking him for advice. "If it doesn't rhyme with Nantucket, I'm probably not going to be able to do that."

"I am accessing variations of poems that meet your specified parameters. Processing. Ninety-eight point three percent of them would likely not be suitable to be sent to your significant other."

"What does it say about me that my girlfriend can't remember what she sees in me and my best friend is a glorified coffee maker?"

Andy puts on his "quizzical" expression. "I have never quite understood the human practice of comparing sophisticated machinery with lesser counterparts. If you would like a coffee, I can certainly download and emulate any number of clips posted online, but I would caution you that in most cases, coffee does not mix well with the quantity of alcoholic beverage you have consumed."

"So, what do you think I should do?"

"Calvin, you perform at your best when you are under significant stress. If you apply this to human mating rituals, you should confront Aphrodite with these problems and refuse to accept any result other than the one you seek."

"That's easier said than done, pal."

"Consider this, friend. Do you bend to the will of the universe or do you make the universe bend to your will?"

That makes a surprising amount of sense, or I'm a little buzzed. I start toward the communications panel, but decide that drunk dialing might not improve my chances.

• • •

I'm hanging out in the break room when Dozer enters. She was the first one to deliver an ass chewing about the Mardi Gras fiasco as it has come to be known. I'm still in a foul mood after Stacy's email showed up saying that we need some "time apart" for things to calm down.

Other than my scheduled patrols, I have kept a low profile and haven't been seen in public. It was the one suggestion Wendy offered that I didn't have a problem with. Some of the others were anatomically impossible.

Sheila sucks in a long breath to get my attention and says, "Stringel, I can't believe I'm doing this, but do you want to come with me today?"

"What?"

"My agency set up an appearance this afternoon. They want you to tag along because the client said his kid is really into armored heroes and you're the closest thing available."

I ignore the slight and say, "A birthday party?"

She smirks. "A rich kid's party. Your cut is fifteen grand for three hours of taking kids up for a flight and maybe firing off some star shells for fireworks."

Five grand an hour? There might be something to this scam She-Dozer has going on. "Alright count me in. Do you do the balloon animals?"

"Up yours, Stringel. Here's the park they've reserved. Meet me there at three and try not to screw this up."

• • •

Wealthy people sure know how to throw a party. The tent is huge with bundles of balloons anchoring each corner. A sign indicates pony rides and it looks like a miniature carnival has been set up.

I'm flying a little slow with the weight of Roller slowing me down. While it wasn't part of the deal, I still want to practice issuing commands to my sidekick. Plus, it'll probably piss off Sheila. That's an added bonus.

Dropping Roller onto the ground, I land on it and look for the adoring partygoers.

Nothing. There's no one here! My paranoia shifts into overdrive and I dial up thermals and sweep for life signs.

A large area force shield slams down over the immediate area. It takes a moment to locate the force field generator crudely disguised as a barbeque. It wouldn't be a problem if several other objects hadn't just powered up. Threat assessment reads four in the tent and two coming from the gaming area.

Magnify.

I lock on to the nearest one. It's about eleven foot tall. Too small to be a Type D Warbot. The face is shaped like a hammerhead shark. The optical receptors on each end are a dead giveaway. I've only seen pictures and crude schematics of these before – Type C Assassin Bots. Two clawed arms and four heavy lasers that spread out in an "X" pattern from its back.

Gee, who might be behind all this? Considering the UN issued a proclamation banning the use of these back in the late nineties when they were sent in and killed that Iraqi dictator … and his sixteen body doubles.

The lasers targeting me can't be bought in an office supply store either. Lazarus isn't pussyfooting around. I sling my mini-gun into the firing position and power it up. At the same time, I issue commands via my neural network.

Roller: Activate all weapons systems. Destroy all hostile targets.

All hell breaks loose. I leap away from Roller and start firing as the six techno-assassins bring their weapons to bear. The area defined by the shield includes precious little cover. Coincidence? I don't think! Frantically, I dig around my mind for the little I know about the Type C model.

The six star shell forty millimeter grenades are fired without concern. The two tear gas rounds will follow after that. I need to jettison all of them to get at the four high explosive armor piercers I keep at the bottom of the magazine. The HEAP rounds should take one out once I punch through some shields.

Roller fires the twin pulse cannons I mounted on it. Twice the amount of firepower a normal B can bring. They knock an attacker to the ground with the first salvo. The second rips into the torso, stitching damage all along the left sides. My mini-gun penetrates the weakened area and set off some explosions. The other five combine their twenty odd lasers to blast me back into the force shield and shave half my shielding off in a single shot.

That's when I realize that the problem and the solution are one in the same. They're all attacking me and ignoring Roller completely. The targeting system they use is single purpose.

Roller: Target Shield Generator. Destroy. Then return to previous order.

I lose another five percent before my robot complies and dodge as best I can while discarding the idea of returning fire.

It takes two shots, but Roller slags the generator. The shield drops and I shoot skyward. They pursue. I feel like that guy Maverick hated in *Top Gun* when all those Russian fighters are hounding him. The best I can do is swiveling my grenade launcher to the rear and use the HEAP rounds to knock them off my six. The four rounds strike home, but are done all too soon.

Sadly my wingman, Roller, is stuck on the ground. My crude solution is to bring them by on a strafing run right next to the twin pulse cannons and let my robot blow one out of the air at a time, all the while reinforcing my shields and hoping Patterson runs out of robots before I run out of protection.

When there are three left, one peels off and begins attacking Roller. Someone updated the targeting parameters. The other two keep pounding me with their lasers. One gets through and damages my jetpack. I plow into the ground and dig a trench thirty feet long. Groggy but desperate, I roll under the tent and blow the supports away with my force blaster. The tent collapses on all of us. The mini-gun is useless, twisted in the crash and I obviously need some system that will keep my force sledge attached during emergency landings. The clawed hands of the assassins rip through the tarp like confetti as the lasers stab like knives looking for a target.

The icon for Roller in the corner of my heads up display is orange with shades of red showing. That means heavy damage. The good news is it has disposed of its opponent and is turning the one remaining cannon on my assailants.

The telemetry I get from Roller pinpoints the Type C's positions. I stumble over and under the furniture to come up behind one. Pouncing, I leap on the back of the machine and bear hug the lasers rendering them useless. Getting another bit of inspiration, I use it as a shield while shooting the remaining one with my force blaster. Between my attacks and Roller's the last one falls and I start ripping the one in my arms to pieces.

The next thing I know, I'm barely awake, spitting up blood, flat on my back and staring up at the sky. It's hard to think straight and after a few minutes my mind is able to piece together what just happened over the warbling of my Master Alarm. The person monitoring the fight triggered the self destruct hoping it would take me out in the process.

It almost did. I'm in a bad way. My arms are functional, but the lower torso is immobilized. Comm gear is out. The neural gear is still working, so I call my wobbling Roller over. With some effort, I crawl onto the robot and attach myself to the non moving part where one remaining pulse cannon is.

Roller: Defensive mode. Take us back to Guardian Headquarters best speed possible.

I suppose we made quite a sight on the Interstate. I don't know for certain because I passed out somewhere along the way.

• • •

With bruised ribs, contusions up and down my legs, and sagging into my wheelchair, José pushes me into the control room. The main screen is split four ways. The other three Guardian groups and the Olympians are all in it.

I focus on Patterson, he's in his armor with the faceplate open. Hazel eyes stare through me, but he doesn't show any emotions.

Wendy is furious. "Would you like to see the telemetry, Andydroid removed from Mechani-Cal's armor again, Lazarus. Either you sanctioned one of my team members or your one hundred percent inventory reported to the UN Security Council is in doubt. Which is it?"

"I've had my people checking on it, young lady. There appear to be irregularities and I will let you know when the investigation is complete."

That sets off people on all four screens. The heavy set black man from Harlem, Bolt Action, is the loudest of them all. The human missile gets so close to the camera in his headquarters that his face fills the screen and I can see the spittle flying out of his mouth. "That kind of irregularity bullshit might fly in front of a congressional panel, but I ain't hearing it, Patterson. You might have put up the money, but the Guardians were my creation! I'll kick your ass out and disband the West Coast unit in a New York minute."

Patterson is way too calm. "Unless you have definitive proof, David, I'd have to cite the bylaws of our charters. I can only be removed if someone from my team calls for a formal investigation," he pauses and looks at all his sycophants. "I don't believe anyone has. Consider this - the scumbag sitting in the wheelchair over there is using hundreds of robots taken from The Evil Overlord in a profiteering scheme. Anyone who has dealt with him knows he spares no expense when he feels he has been crossed. Since we know he has the capability to manufacture his own A, B, and D units, it can be assumed that he can also do the same with the C series. So keep that in mind before you rush to judge."

"Then, why don't you submit to an impartial telepathic scan and remove all doubt?" Bolt Action has the stones to call the mighty Lazarus out. Even through my discomfort, I can appreciate that.

"Whatever happened to innocent until proven guilty? Besides, I can't in good faith allow a telepath to look at my thoughts because of all the proprietary information about Promethia in my mind. You'll have to take my word on it."

Wendy takes his word, chews it up and spits it right back at him. "Sheila was supposed to be there until she suddenly got a text message saying her boyfriend had been in a car accident and was at the emergency room. Would The Overlord give a rat's ass about collateral damage? Come after my team again, Ultraweapon and you better plan on dealing with me."

"Wendy, I know you're new as a leader, but you can't take every injury personally. These things happen. We're in a dangerous business." Patterson couldn't sound more condescending if he tried.

Obviously, Ultraweapon has his plausible deniability lined up. Nothing anyone does here today will change a damn thing. The sad part is my deal with Florida helps him out. I chuckle, but it comes out as a grunt. Wendy turns toward me and says, "Do you want to address the body? As the aggrieved party, you have that right?"

I glare at Patterson and say, "The Overlord hasn't shown his face since the bug invasion. There's every chance he's dead, but it doesn't matter. Either you or him wasted somewhere in the neighborhood of a hundred million dollars to try and off me and it didn't work. Whoever it is will get what's coming to them. I promise."

Patterson doesn't flinch. Instead he smiles and says, "I hope you get better soon, Stringel. It's been a long time since you worked for me, but I wish nothing but success to all current and former Promethia employees."

I spin the chair around and roll toward the exit. "I'm sure you do. Now, if you'll excuse me, I'll be fixing my armor. See you around soon, Lazarus."

"We should do lunch. Call my people."

"When I do drop by, it'll be a surprise visit."

Andy and four José clones join me in the workshop and tell me to sit tight and give them directions. Andydroid I can count on and José is happy that someone is actually taking his clone powers seriously and trying to help him become a better hero. We have to cannibalize one of the three "El Cheapo" suits I've been making for the Six Pack. The irony is that those suit designs are the same ones that were going to make me a multimillionaire when Vicky and I were planning to ride off into the sunset. Roller is in bad shape. The second pulse cannon is shot and I don't have a replacement. I'll have to put something else in there instead, but I do make a command decision to put the missile mount on Floater. With limited armor and little shielding, it only really gets one shot. I might as well make the most of it. While I'm on the subject, I'm not going to carry any stinking tear gas or other useless grenades any more. It's high explosive all the way from here on out.

The screen in the workshop lights up and Stacy's face appears on it. She looks around the room and says, "Guys can I have a private word with Cal?"

I've got a good idea what's coming and have no plans on making it easier for her. "Whatever's on your mind, Aphrodite, just say it."

If she notices that I didn't call her Stacy, she doesn't show it. "I told Lazarus that you and I aren't seeing each other anymore."

"I'm glad he was informed before I was."

"Be reasonable, Cal. It's for the best. I'm not the woman that fell for you. He'll drop this vendetta he has, now."

I shake my head and say, "For someone who has been in the business as long as you have, you're an idiot."

"Cal, you're upset and lashing out. You need to calm down."

Cutting her off, I say, "You just don't get it. Patterson has a god complex. In his mind, he is incapable of failure and he just failed to kill me. I'm on his list of things 'to do' now. He wouldn't let it go even if you offered to marry his ass tomorrow, but you're right about not being the woman I loved. She had a spine and was ten times the hero you'll ever be!"

With that, I cut the screen off not wanting to hear another word from her. The Stacy that was mindwiped wouldn't recognize the one she's become.

• • •

Five days later, I'm cleaning up after my first patrol in my new armor. For a change, things went well and the repaired armor performed nicely even up against a massive pile up on Interstate 10. There're a couple of things I need to tweak, but I'm too tired to do it. I just want a shower. I'm pulling some fresh underwear out of my drawers when there is a knock at my door.

"Who is it?"

"Wendy."

"Hold on a sec," I yank the dirty shorts from around my ankles back up. "Come on in."

She's in some robes. "What did you want, Mechani-Cal?"

"Huh?"

"You buzzed me a minute ago and said it's important."

"I don't think so..."

She yelps in pain and grabs at her neck. Writhing in pain, she rips off her necklace and tosses it to the ground.

I'm rushing to her and trying to process what the hell just happened when something washes over me. It's like I'm in a fog, everything is blurry except Wendy. It was like I'd never really seen her before … so desirable. Everything I've always wanted.

Wendy seems to have forgotten about the burn to her neck and she stares at me. The tip of her tongue flicks across her lips as her hands unknot the sash, freeing her from her robes. A flimsy nightdress is all that's underneath and seconds later it's around her ankles. A gust of wind lifts the two of us into the air and tosses us on my bed. Her smile matches my own.

• • •

Hours later, I come to my senses. I'm exhausted, battered and have a splitting headache. My bruises from the battle with Patterson's assassins have bruises on top of them. The sheets are stained with the blood from the scratch marks Wendy left on my back. There's no mirror nearby, but I'm sporting at least one black eye.

The fog is lifting and what just happened is starting to piece itself together. A minute ago, she had her hands around my throat and was choking me.

"Wendy? Are you okay?"

"I think you broke my nose," she says cupping her face.

"Sorry. What just happened?"

"I don't …," she starts and then winces tracing a bloody line across her throat where the new scar from her necklace was. "My necklace … then you … Mather! That sonnuvabitch Mather! He was controlling us!"

Stumbling out of bed, I say, "Get cleaned up. I'm getting into my armor in case he tries again."

I stop as something catches my eye. There's an item sticking out of my vent. Wendy sees what I'm pointing at and uses her powers to bring the vent and a chunk of the ceiling down. It's a small surveillance bot with a now broken high resolution camera and transmitter attached – high tech gear made for the CIA by the industrious folks at Promethia.

Ten minutes later, everyone is in the monitor room. The inside of my armor smells like blood and sex. I'm not amused.

"Mount Olympus is offline," Sheila says. "I can't raise anyone."

"Andydroid, Cal, you're with me," Wendy says. Her nose is covered by one of those bandages and the four necklaces around her neck make her look like she's shooting a rap video.

"I should come to," Sheila says.

"No," Wendy hisses. "Andy's immune, Cal's armor should protect him, and I don't have any more necklaces to spare. Stay here and run things."

She-Dozer opens her mouth to say something, but wisely shuts it when she sees the look on WhirlWendy's face. I'm more than prepared to do something rash, but so is the other victim of this.

"Be careful," Chain Charmer says.

"I'm going to wring his skinny neck!" Wendy replies. "Cal, Andy, let's get to the jet. Andy, start doing preflight and get us priority clearance with the FAA. I want to be airborne in ten minutes. Sheila, get Bolt Action on the line and tell him what's going on."

Two hours is a lot of time in the air to simmer about things. I link up and check the internet. Wendy and I are already all over it. The PR people arrive at our headquarters and contact us on the jet to formulate a plan. Wendy disconnects them. Mather's little perverse act will damage her carefully crafted reputation. It will cost her millions of dollars and fans as well. I have no real reputation worth speaking of, but no one uses me and gets away with it.

After landing at Dulles, I have a hard time keeping up with Wendy as we fly to Mount Olympus. True I'm carrying Andy, but she's flying much faster than I've ever seen her before.

Ares, Apollo, and Athena are out front arguing with her when I arrive and deposit Andy on the walkway.

"Go back to New Orleans, Wendy. Take your team with you. We have the problem under control."

"Where's Mather?" I ask. I've already brought the mini-gun around at them and spin the barrels to let them know I'm serious.

Athena ignores me, probably knowing I don't want to listen to anything she has to say. "Wendy, letting you all in there isn't going to help the situation. It's only going to make things worse. We're not letting you in and if Stringel tries, he's going to get beaten to a pulp."

Wendy looks down at the pavement and I can almost see her resolve fading. I start planning how I can take all three Olympians in the quickest way possible when the young woman from Staten Island speaks. Her eyes come up and I can sense the power washing off of her in waves. The wind rises and my suits barometer takes a nosedive as a vortex forms around our small group. "Cal isn't your problem, Crenshaw. I am. Get out of my way or I will rip your damn clubhouse off its foundations!"

Ares steps toward Wendy, but I hit him with a two second burst from my gun and it knocks him back. Wendy's gust of wind tosses Apollo aside like a stuntman in a bad Hollywood movie.

All that's left is a thunderstruck Athena. She backs away, holding one of her energy spears defensively. "This is the wrong move Wendy, and you know it."

We pass her by and I swivel my head and look at the so-called goddess of wisdom. "Take a look at what a real leader looks like, Athena."

Andy is updating me on what happened from accessing the Olympian's database. Mather used the amplifier designed by Promethia and the absence of the most powerful Olympians to take his revenge on Wendy and try to subjugate the rest of Athena's team. Apparently, he'd been working his mojo on Hestia for the last few weeks, but then included Hera so her force fields could protect him while he held court over his new thralls.

Aphrodite was able to resist. The thralls captured her and dragged my ex down to the cells. Along the way she used her psionic blasts to knock out a series of electrical panels. The power to the chair only lasted another thirty minutes before it failed and left the Emperor on his throne with literally no clothes on and a bunch of pissed off Olympians around him.

• • •

"So look who decided to show up," Mather says from behind the barrier. "Did the two of you have a good time?"

"Why Mather?"

"Why what, Wendy? Why did I do it? Because I could. You've been on that high horse so long that someone needs to knock you off of it. You walk around pretending to be little Miss Perfect, but you're not. You're a dirty stinking little whore and it was my pleasure to make sure the world saw you for what you really are. Why this chump? I suppose I could have picked the wetback and let you have a six way, but Stringel here is the biggest embarrassment on your roster. I thought it was fitting. Besides he never deserved Aphrodite to begin with."

"I'm guessing Patterson hooked you up with the gear."

The sneering little shit grins. "Nah, you'd like that wouldn't you, Stringbean. I thought he could use an early birthday present. You're a laughingstock, Stringel and not even worth his time. Too bad the chair cut out when it did; I was getting to the best part. You weren't just going to have a sex tape. The grand finale was going to be a snuff film."

Wendy cuts into his tirade and says, "You're going to have a long time to think about it, Mather."

"Probably not. You see, I've been giving it a lot of thought. I think that amplifier overwhelmed my abilities and it drove me a little off the deep end. It's all the chair's fault. With some time and therapy, I'm sure I'll be okay again. I just need some me time in a quiet place to come to grips with the things I did."

The smug bastard isn't even bothering to act.

Wendy is spitting mad. She's had a rough night and doesn't deserve to see where this is going to end up. Something like this would eat her up inside. Me? It'll be a nibble or two on my soul. I might lose a couple of hours of sleep on this, but that's it. I put my armored hand on her shoulder. My force blaster takes out the security camera. "Go back upstairs. I'll finish up down here. You don't need to see this."

She looks at me. Realization sets in. This isn't her domain, despite what just happened, she's a hero. "Cal, maybe it doesn't have to be like this. You don't have to do this."

"Yeah, I do. Just go, Wendy."

She walks out the door and stops, looking over her shoulder before leaving.

I turn to Michael Mather. "You shouldn't have included me in this. That was a big mistake."

"I'm so scared, tough guy."

I drop the barrier separating us and step into his cell. "That's another mistake. Any last words?"

"You're not going to do it."

"I'm not an embarrassment, Mather. I'm a villain and not one of you 'turn the other cheek' chumps. You might be right about that amplifier overwhelming you. It's what probably triggered your heart attack."

My palms crackle with power and the air surrounding smells like ozone. Volts don't kill. Amps do and everyone knows that it doesn't take too much to do it.

Mather's powers fueled by his fear put a strain on my shields, but he's worn out from trying to control the Olympians. His futile attacks and screams last only long enough for me to grab him and turn on the juice.

Most of the Olympians are waiting for me when I come back upstairs. Aphrodite won't even look at me. Athena wants to run her mouth, but it's Ares who speaks, "You shouldn't have killed him, Mechanical. That's not the way to do things in our world. People like you should be in jail."

"Screw your world! Go ahead and try to lock me up. I'll make certain that the whole world knows what you folks can do with that chair. I'll squeal like a stuck pig. You won't be able to shut me up. Don't bother trying to mindwipe me, I've already taken precautions. I'll let them know all your dirty deals and the stuff that you heroes want hidden from the public. What were you going to do, let Mather off with a slap on the wrist? He all but raped Wendy and admitted that he was going to make her kill me live on the internet if the chair hadn't cut out."

"Do whatever you want, Olympians," Wendy follows right behind my proclamation. "My team is leaving. Cover it up. Whitewash it. You have a knack for that Athena. But, if you arrest him, I'll put my money out there to defend him and it will get ugly. I promise you."

It's nice to have the backing of a powerful person for a change.

She doesn't say anything else until we're on the tarmac. "Take the jet back to New Orleans. I'm taking some personal time. Tell Sheila she's in charge."

"Are you okay, Wendy?"

"No. I'm not. I helped you kill a man tonight. I'm not even sure I deserve to be a leader."

"Superhuman doesn't mean you're no longer human. He was the one with the loaded gun. It just ended up shooting him instead. The world might not be a better place without him, but it isn't any worse."

She wipes some tears from her eyes as Andy gets the jet going. "You're not upset about it, Cal."

"I'm a little worked up, but it'll pass. Go, get yourself together and come back when you are ready."

"What about you?"

I open my face plate and give her a smile. "I lived in denial so long I've got a timeshare there. If they ask me whether it was me and you, I'll deny everything and then I'll insult them. Like you'd ever sleep with me!"

She laughs weakly and then is swept upwards in a gust of wind. I'm suddenly tired. After all this joking about sex tapes, by some fluke of fate, I have two with a pair of the most powerful women on the planet. That's quite an accomplishment for a gangly looking guy with stringy hair that always looks a little greasy. I should wear my shame with pride.

So why don't I feel that proud right now?

Chapter Nine

Sic Semper Tyrannosaurus

Bolt Action contacts us and interviews everyone about the incident, he asked every member if they wanted to suspend me from the team and launch a formal inquest, my teammates stood up for me. I'd already shown all of them the tape of Mather taunting us with what was going to happen if the chair hadn't cut out on him. They don't go to the mat for me. They do it for Wendy. I know it, but appreciate it just the same.

My turn comes and I stare down the angry man and his graying crew cut. I'm ready for the ex-Marine sniper to try ripping me a new one, but his demeanor changes abruptly.

"Stringel, you're no hero. Got no character. I can just tell. Some people got it. You don't. We should drum you out before you do even more damage to our reputation, but it ain't gonna happen today. I love that little girl like she was my own daughter. She thought I was holding her back, but I was trying to protect her. Something like this would've never happened if she was still up here! That Mather bastard wouldn't have had the balls to try it. You ... you saved me the trouble of killing him myself."

"You're welcome," I say.

"I wasn't thanking you. 'Sides, we both know Patterson's gunning for you. Ain't shit I can really do about it until he tries again, but I'm betting this time he'll come in person. All I can say is be ready for him."

"Maybe I'll go looking for him," I say.

The man throws his head back and laughs. When he stops, he says, "Look into a mirror and say that line again. See if it sounds just as stupid to you. If it comes down to it, I'm hoping you take each other out and I'm rid of two problems."

The vote of confidence in my abilities is astounding.

As the screen goes blank, Andy enters. "I detected the transmission terminated and would like to resume monitor duty."

"You don't think any less of me do you?" I ask Andydroid.

"In empirical terms," Andy begins, "all human life is equal. Given that Mather's endgame involved Wendy killing you, the loss of life appeared inevitable. This negates scenarios where you do not kill him as it can be assumed he would try again, based on the evidence you provided."

"Okay," I say, waiting to see where he's going with this.

"Therefore, your life and Wendy's life must be weighed against the life of Mather. Based on data gathered, MindOver had a longer career as a hero, so on the basis of time and missions, he would have the advantage over you, but not Miss La Guardia. However, your previous actions resulted in world salvation and, on a personal note, my reactivation. The conclusion is subjective on my part, but your life is more valuable than Mister Mather's."

I have my own opinion and it's pretty damn subjective as well. Still, it's nice to see someone agree with me.

"Thanks Andy, I appreciate it."

• • •

The furor over my streaming sex life dies down after three weeks. Something else eventually replaces it, though I did enjoy the catcalls from those overweight, clinging to the good years of their life, guys down on the beach after my rematch with Seawall. They came over and cheered me on and asked me how it felt to be "windblown."

I laugh it off and tell them it's a fake and that I wish. On the positive front, no one has shown up to arrest me yet. The relations between the Gulf Coast and the other major teams in North America are downright chilly, but I really don't care. It's not like I'm interested in a transfer, but I don't stay idle. I design an overloaded powercell launcher based on the rifle I used in the fight in Missouri. It ends up looking more like a World War Two bazooka – a one-time weapon that fires an energy capsule rigged to explode. Ultraweapon's shields will probably stop it, but they'll take a pounding.

I'm also trading out the sledge that never really lived up to my hopes for it. I have a maul and am working on it. There's no force field this time. Instead, I have an electrical capacitor with enough juice to light up a couple of city blocks.

As I'm putting the finishing touches on it, Charmer bursts into my workshop. "Kimodo is in trouble. She needs our help."

I bite back my sarcastic response and simply nod. Kimodo is a big disappointment. She's constantly in over her head. My initial impression that she was good was way off base. I set the maul down and jog to the monitor room.

"Villain is way too powerful for me alone. Send help immediately. He's coming for ..." The lizard woman shrieks into her communicator before the connection is broken.

Andydroid brings up the coordinates from her transmission. It's about thirty or forty minutes north in a small parish that, like much of Louisiana, is by a swamp. Meanwhile, Sheila is already formulating our plan of attack. She won't admit it, but she relishes being the temporary leader until Wendy returns.

"We don't know what we're in for, or who the villain is. There's nothing in our database for anyone known to be operating out of that area, so we're going in blind. We'll take the hoversleds. The jet would get us there quicker, but we might have a hard time finding a spot to land and I don't want to leave anyone on pilot duty. José Prime, you're on monitor. Alert the other teams to our situation. Cal, bring that damn ball robot you're always going on about. All the rest of you stay sharp."

Chain Charmer hands The Bugler the spare necklace and Bo transforms into his "Bat Bugler" form. He even learned how to fly, though not really that well yet.

Me? I actually figured out what it does for me ... languages. Of all the stupid effin' abilities! A couple of the José clones were jabbering on in Spanish too fast for me to follow more than a couple words when Jin let me try it on again and suddenly I could understand them perfectly. I asked Jin to say something in Japanese, which really pissed him off since I didn't know the difference between Japanese and his Chinese ancestry. To make a long and somewhat embarrassing story short, he cussed me out in Mandarin and I understood every word of it. José even grabbed one of his Mexican porn mags and I could read the stories.

Watching Bo sprout wings, sonar sight, and battle claws makes me feel like I got the short end of the stick. In other words, I felt all too normal.

Me and the two José clones with suits don our armor. The three other versions of him attach Floater to one of the hoversleds while I grab a fueled jet pack and summon Roller. It is still a pulse cannon down, but after the next payday, I might be able to turn up the parts for a replacement from a person that I used to do some "work" for.

Grabbing the pommels I lift Roller into the air and get a head start. Carrying the load means I'll fly slower, but without our leader and most powerful member, Sheila likes to err on the side of caution. Even though I don't like her that much, I respect that attitude. It keeps the repairs on my suit down to less than what they would be otherwise.

• • •

They're just getting off their sleds as I arrive and release Roller. The pommels retract and the internal gyroscope starts the robot moving. I flex my tired arms. Forty-three minutes in the same position can do that to a person. Next, I activate Floater and get it airborne.

Sheila and Andy try to raise Kimodo, but there's no luck there. Even I actually get a bit concerned. Yeah, I'm an asshole and all that, but I do have a heart. It might be a couple of sizes too small like that character on the Christmas specials, but it should be noted for the record that I don't wish harm on any of my teammates … usually.

"Fan out, locate Kim and any other persons in danger. Andy isn't detecting anything on the police wire for this place. In fact, he isn't picking up any transmissions other than our own. Andy, use Cal's scouter and look for thermals. Jin, the clinic is over that way about a mile and a half. Check it out and then hit the fire and the police stations. From the map, it looks like they're right next to each other. Armored Josés, there's a cluster of churches in that direction. Cal, me, and the rest will move toward the two schools in this place."

It's a good plan. People are somewhat predictable. In times like these, locals tend to congregate around schools, hospitals, and churches.

Andy finally gets thermal readings outside the junior high school gym on the baseball field. It looks like the whole town is there along with several things that are seriously big. Their silhouettes match things from my childhood toy box - dinosaurs! There's a big one, probably a T-Rex along with a Triceratops and a Stegosaurus if I remember my plastic toys right. The people are herded in the middle, but looked like they're not being eaten at the moment.

As the rest of the group displays their own incredulous looks at facing things long since extinct, I don't mind the idea of capturing a live dinosaur and wonder how much a zoo might pay for something like that.

Bless my mercenary heart!

After calling the groups checking out the other spots, Sheila has us make a cautious approach. Andy moves Floater to just behind the right field fence. In the darkness, it's hard to pick out Kim, but it looks like she's prone on the ground by an object situated on the pitcher's mound. All the other people are sitting. There's a soft hum, like chanting.

"I don't like this," Bo says.

"Jin, your magic chains won't break, so you tie up T-Rex's hind legs. Sanford, dose it with your paralyzing juice and see how much it takes to knock it out. Cal takes the horned one, and I have the one with the big tail, just try to restrain them and keep them away until Sanford can render them harmless. The rest of you get to the people and evacuate them this way. Cal, move your other robot through the parking lot and point it at the swamp. If there are any reinforcements, they'll be coming that way, since we haven't seen any on our way up here.

For a minute, we hit those reptiles better than any other super group could. The Gulf Coast Guardians are a finely tuned machine! I'm locking horns with an honest to goodness Triceratops and feel the ground shake as the massive T-Rex goes to the ground. Sheila has the front end of her dinosaur pushed up and it can't whip its tail around without toppling over.

It's a thing of utter beauty. If Andy had time to hack the scoreboard, I'd have him change it to Heroes: 3, Dinosaurs: 0.

My mental victory lap grinds to a screeching halt when I hear one of the clones exclaim, "*Madre Dios*, they've all been turned into lizard people."

Bugler is trying to pull a pair of them to their feet when they spin on him and drive him to the ground and more leap on him in a semi-reptilian rugby scrum. The unarmored clones knock a few out with their stun batons before they are swarmed under.

Fear of the unknown is one of my weaknesses. It's something that makes my heart go pitter patter and I've got a bad feeling. No one is sure whether or not Mangler is alive. Is it possible that he's refined his process? Or is this something else? The lizard people drag the clones and Bugler to their feet with clawed hands placed directly on the throat. Back at the base, José will suffer a lot of pain if one of his clones is killed, but he will eventually grow another one. We can't really grow another Biloxi Bugler.

Kim rises. She's decked out in bird feathers like some whacked out cult priestess and I don't need that alien dude from the movies screaming, "It's a trap!" to spot one. She says, "The Master comes!"

"Anemone, go!" Sheila shouts.

Sanford Marley Acojo, named after the great reggae singer and Red Foxx's junk dealing funny man, springs into action. His pressurized spray jets would make a backyard water fighter drool with envy reaching up to one hundred feet. Our captives will get immobilized along with the lizard folks, but hopefully no blood will be shed.

I'm already moving forward as the crystalline thing on the pitcher's mound shimmers and something steps out. It's some kind of portal.

Without any evidence of a power supply, I have to classify it as magic. I'm expecting another lizard man, but he's not. He, or it, is further along.

"So these are the mammals that would dare challenge me!" His hiss booms in my mind like telepathy. My bad juju meter goes into overdrive and I throw caution to the wind, chucking forty millimeter high explosive at his ass a cutting loose with the mini. Darts of plasma energy spatter against some kind of shield and my grenades disappear in a series of pathetic poofs.

Anemone screams, "Suck on this, mon!" and shoots thin streams of paralytic juice at this Master thing. With a wave of its clawed hand, the liquid forms into a ball which is sent spinning into She-Dozer and Chain Charmer. They both spasm and collapse.

Shit! Our team is going down fast.

"Hit him with everything you've got!" I bark to the remaining Guardians. The serpent's magical shield absorbs all the punishment we can throw at it. Grenades vaporize, bolts of plasma and stun rays do nothing and all through it, I hear this mocking laughter in my mind!

"Yes! Show me your power. Display your might and let me demonstrate how useless it is."

A three clawed hand snaps out and some kind of purplish energy slams into one of the clone's suits. It topples over and then seconds later is joined by the other José.

Andy is hit and he stumbles forward before freezing in place. My thermal imagery shows that all his power systems suddenly went off line. I call José at the base and tell him to get reinforcements before a bolt hits me too. I struggle up to one knee but everything stops.

The suit's systems lock up. The master alarm beeps for a second and dies a mute death. I can still see out my clear faceplate and look down at my hand that was trying to push me upright. In the limited light produced by the villain's crystal portal gizmo, the metal is different.

Stone?

Stone?

Stone!

I'm stuck inside an effin' statue. He ruined my suit! I'm going to kill him!

"You think too loudly, mammal. All of you do! My name is unpronounceable to your, flat, ill-formed tongues, but you can call me Tyrannosorcerer Rex! I have awakened from my long slumber and will return this world to reptilian rule."

The lunatic goes on to bitch about his people rebelling against him until he called down the sky to slay all the traitors. Part of me is stunned. This whack job exterminated the dinosaurs and created the Gulf of Mexico? No effin' way!

"Oh, so you doubt my power, eh mammal? Was not reverting your metal to the base stone it came from enough to make you realize what you face? I see a further demonstration is in order. He waves his claw and Anemone enters my limited field of vision encased in some kind of translucent egg.

"Watch apeling. Watch the birth of my new race!"

Sanford begins quivering. The "egg" hatches and he falls out. Parts of him are bursting out of his costume. The gruesome event takes maybe two minutes, or a lifetime to play out while the lizard people near me sway and chant. The only thing good about it is that voice in my head is gone. Rex has his head pointed to the sky and is hissing to the beat of his faithful. Eventually one of those poison spitting dinosaurs from that one movie stands up where my teammate was. It approaches Rexxie and bends its head allowing the sorcerer to grasp it with a three clawed hand.

With my suit's evacuation systems also turned to stone, I feel urine running down my right leg and collecting at the knee.

"Now for the strong female. She will make a good mate for my other great servant and will breed a new generation of mammal killers. Your turn will come soon."

As the presence leaves my mind, I search for anything that might help. In the faraway darkness, I see the shape of Roller. I give it the command to move toward me. It does! My neural net is still up. The powercell at the base of my neck is still intact. That means I can still control Floater as well. I just can't see it.

I don't have much time. Sheila is already beginning her transformation and I could be next. I'll attack from both sides. Floater goes first with missiles and then acting as a distraction. Roller will come in from the back. Will the pulse cannon be able to breach that shield? Screw it! I'll detonate Roller at the bleachers behind home plate. Some of the shrapnel will have to get through.

I issue my orders and do something I never do … pray.

Sheila's transformation is interrupted at the midpoint by twin darts of light. The serpent sorcerer barely gets up his shield in time and the impact causes him to stumble on his thick legs. There's a quick burst of light as Floater explodes and I grimace from the feedback.

The villain's presence slams down on my mind, ripping at the fabric of my existence and I scream right through Roller's explosion. The blast hurls people backward and shatters that crystal portal. My ears won't stop ringing and all through it, I pray that this thing dies. I make bargains with gods I've never heard of. I even promise not to watch soft core porn ever again.

In the middle of all this, I'm knocked over. I can still see straight ahead, but the angle has changed. The dust clears and I see Tyrannosorcerer Rex still standing behind his shield. *No! No! No!*

Slowly, he turns in my direction and my life is flashing before my eyes. I'm going to die. This is it.

The mage rears back and I prepare for the burst of energy that will finish me, but nothing comes. Rex wobbles and claws at his chest for a few seconds. Then, he drops to the ground and nothing. I can't see any movement.

• • •

Time passes. There are intermittent screams of pain and moaning, but no other sounds. Mosquitoes land on my face and feast. I call out, but there is no answer.

Finally, when I don't think I can handle it anymore, Sheila appears. She staggers to over to Rex first, vomits and approaches. Sheila hefts me with ease. Putting me down like some kind of stupid lawn gnome, we look at each other. If she's noticed that she's pretty much naked, she doesn't show it.

"Cal, are you okay?" she whispers.

"My suit's been turned to stone! You?"

"No need to scream. I turned back. Sanford did as well. What happened?"

"I got Roller as close as I could and then activated the self-destruct. Is the bad guy dead?"

"Yeah, it's weird though, there're some chunks of him ripped out, like they were never there. Listen, there are a lot of people injured and I think Kim is dead. I'm going to run back to my sled and get help. Do you need me to bust you out of there?"

"No! No! Give it some time, maybe it'll turn back like you did," I probably sound a bit whiny there, but this is my suit we're talking about! Desperation is in order.

Left alone with only the cries of the injured to keep me company, I postulate on what happened. The crystal portal was outside of his shield. If the pieces of it were still active, they might have transported chunks of the reptile away, leaving him resembling an unfinished jigsaw puzzle. The scenario reminds me of that Croce song from the seventies.

Technically, we won, but I won't feel happy until my suit is back to normal. I already sacrificed my two robots.

• • •

Forty-five minutes later and happiness hasn't shown up yet. I'm still an effin' lawn ornament. The higher powers that granted my requests felt necessary to exact a price.

"Give it up, Cal. It's not happening." Sheila says.

"Just five more minutes. Please," I sound like a kid being told to get off their game console and go to sleep.

"Andy isn't changing back. Neither of the José suits are turning back, and I'm sorry to say this, but your suit isn't going to either."

I sigh in defeat. "Go ahead."

She takes her time, so as not to hurt me. "Are you crying?"

"It's dust in my eyes. Shut up!"

When the front chest piece comes off, it's like my heart breaking.

• • •

Andydroid stands motionless in the corner of the workshop. His face locked in a curious, but horrified expression, ironic in the fact that he never really showed that emotion. Kimodo did die and we pretend to mourn a teammate that turned out to be a Mata Hari in our midst. No one else on the team died, but the Bugler's legs were broken and he's out of the game for a time. We had a couple of mystic types in to look at Andy and the other goodies we recovered from Rex's hidden lair. Only one had a solution for my best buddy and it was to turn the body into a golem that would answer orders. Most of them were interested in thumbing through the stuff we brought back and a couple of them made some offers, but I declined based on the idea that maybe I could find something in there that could help Andy. Also, I think some of them were lowballing me.

The strangest thing coming out of this is that when the T-Rex reverted back into a human, it was none other than Hillbilly Bobby. Who'd have thought? Guess that explains why he disappeared. It added a whole new layer of "ewwww" to the mating T-Rex plan because Bobby and Sheila are second cousins. But even that odd fact doesn't lift me out of the mood that I'm wallowing in and I wondered if Bobby was going to try and get his base back from me.

My misery is compounded by discovering that even with a loan from Wendy, I'm having problems getting parts for a new set of armor. I've managed to locate enough synth-muscle to wire a leg. That's about it.

Someone is paying top dollar for all the things I need and making it impossible to locate synth-muscle and the command and control circuitry. I can only imagine who it is. Yeah right. Patterson and his company smell blood and in a not so shocking turn of events, a new armored villain named the RoboDestroyer surfaced in Florida and destroyed every single Type A I had there. Nothing else! Just my bots and source of income.

Petty much!

With no other alternative, I walk out of the workshop and into the monitor room and let them marvel at my inventiveness.

"What's with the get up?" José says, trying and failing not to laugh.

"ManaCALes two point oh," I say. "Twin wrist mounted force blasters, lightweight jet pack, Kevlar suit, helmet, and force field vest. It's the best I can come up with."

I might as well be naked against even a dolt like Seawall, but it's something. Hell, I'm back where I started when the Bugler was kicking my ass.

Sheila inspects me, shrugs, welcomes me back to active duty, and gives me my patrol assignment.

Two hours into it, I'm sitting on an ambulance gurney with a paramedic looking at my arm. The three bank robbers' semi-automatic weapons fire brought down my limited shielding in less than a minute and I took a round in the left arm. Pissed off, I blew a hole the size of my wrist through one of them and the other two dropped their weapons like they were on fire.

"You're a new guy right?" The EMT asks me.

I answer her dumbly, "Yeah, I suppose."

"Listen, maybe this is a wakeup call. Maybe you aren't supposed to be doing this. I'm not trying to be cruel or anything, but you ought to think about a different line of work."

Searching my mind, I can't come up with a decent argument. To sum things up, at the end of the Bug invasion, I had a cool suit, the girl, and a bright future. Now, I have a judgmental paramedic, a stinging pain in my arm, a costume that I would have laughed at, and no girl at all.

Yeah, my future is so very bright right now.

Chapter Ten

Vindication Never Tasted So Bad

"West Coast reporting everything is normal," Patterson knows when my shifts are and calls in his team's status personally. He does this on purpose just to screw with me. Without Andy, we've all had to pick up the slack on monitor duty.

"Gulf Coast reporting everything normal," I answer.

"Tell Wendy, I said welcome back."

"I will Ultraweapon. Are we done?" I reach to sever the connection.

"For tonight we are, Stringel. Sleep tight."

• • •

We all turn up, even Bugler in a wheel chair, to greet Wendy in the monitor room. I accept a hug and a peck on the cheek from the tiny tornado maker.

"It will get better Cal," she whispers in my ear. "I promise."

It's a tiny beam of sunshine over my otherwise drab reality. I cling to it like a lifeline.

Sheila still lets me patrol, but usually pairs me up with Chain Charmer. It's kept me from further injuries, but her lack of faith in my new abilities has plunged to an all time low.

After Wendy's first meeting back, I am approached by the newly reduced in rank She-Dozer. "My agent is on the phone. Someone wants to meet with you."

"Does Patterson really think I'd fall for that again?"

"No it's legit. We established a code phrase that changes so I know it's really him. The client says his name is Paul West. He says you know him from the old days. Do you?"

It takes a second and then I put a name with the face. Paul was the buyer that replaced Vicky after she died. I feel strangely uncomfortable. "Yeah, I know him."

"Okay, I'll have my agent text you his contact information and you can decide if you want to meet up with him. Let us know where and when and we can tag along if necessary."

"I'll do that." I lie. I can't picture myself saying, "Hey guys, I'm about to go meet with The Evil Overlord's chief weapons buyer. Anybody wanna come?"

Now it just remains to be seen what Paul wants with me.

• • •

"Thank you for taking this meeting, Mister Stringel. It's been a long time, but you look well." We meet at a nondescript café in the French Quarter. I want a crowd around that I can lose myself in since I'm "incognito." I've got my force blasters under the baggy shirt I'm wearing and the vest as well. It ain't much, but I'm a pretty fast runner.

"I've been better. How are things with you?"

"There's been a ... how to say this, a downturn for my employer, but things are looking brighter every day."

"I didn't think for a second that he was dead."

"Very astute as always, Mister Stringel." He tips his cup of coffee to me and then sips.

"So what's this all about?"

"A certain person seems to enjoy toying with your life. Isn't that true? You find that even with money, you cannot acquire the things needed to construct a new suit."

"Yes."

"And that same person has a long history of making things difficult for my superior. Does he not?"

"Very true."

"Then we have established some common ground. My superior would like to keep that person occupied pursuing petty vendettas while he is seeing to his holdings, consolidating matters, and awaiting the proper time to rejoin society."

I wonder what Overlord is up to, but it's not like I'm in any position to stop him. "What does this have to do with me?"

He pushes a pad of paper. "I have been instructed to be your benefactor. Write the items you require on this sheet and I will see to it that you receive them as soon as possible."

Too many times I've been burnt by things that sound too good to be true. "What's the catch?"

"Your mere existence infuriates the man who has caused my superior so much grief. Is that not enough for you? I guess not. In that case, my superior has asked that you grant him a future consideration should he require your services."

"I don't think that would go over terribly well given my current employment situation," I reply, since we are talking in circles at the moment. "What about the robots that were destroyed?"

"Those old relics were expendable. My superior was rather impressed at your industrious use for them. He can recognize talented individuals. Pity they have been removed. Regarding the service request, perhaps if it were limited to the downfall of our mutual adversary it would be more palatable?"

My flexible morals are out on display executing a floorshow an Olympic gymnast would envy. Do I trust the Overlord? Hell no! He's not a conventional supervillain. He has the power to detect when people lie to him and not much more, but he uses it with a savage ruthlessness that allows him to gain influence over people and plant spies or agents wherever he wants. He deals in favors and doesn't hesitate to call them in when he needs something.

Would accepting make me any different from someone like Athena, who's willing to give someone like me the shaft on a moment's notice? No. Then again, I never have pretended to be anything other than myself. A new suit will help extend my life expectancy, increase my value to the Guardians, and piss off Ultraweapon … though I'm not sure which order those last two should be in.

I take the pen and begin writing with a speed that might even amaze Hermes. "Deal!"

• • •

"Where did you get the parts?" Wendy asks sneaking up and scaring the crap out of me. Synth-muscle and control circuits are spread all over the place. It's halted my quest to find a solution for Andy. I've discovered that I am very "limited" in my magical potential, but there are various augments that could make me marginally stronger. My research and efforts to this point had allowed me to push a screw a few feet across a table and make it come back. Next week, I'll move on to card tricks!

"I found another cache that used to belong to the Evil Overlord. Now, they're mine." I can still lie to her, but it isn't as easy as it used to be. Technically, this is more of a half-truth. All this hanging around with heroes has made me soft.

"Well, I'm glad you're on your way to making a new suit of armor. It might even make what I'm about to say easier."

Several things cross my mind in that instant. "At least give me my last two weeks pay. It's been fun being a Guardian and I'll miss you most of all."

She laughs at my humor. "Stop. It's not that."

"Well as long as you're not carrying my kid, whatever it is can't be that bad."

There's a very, shall we say, pregnant pause. If Mather wasn't already dead, I'd dig him back up and finish him for good.

"I'm sorry, Cal. Forget I mentioned it."

Fix this Cal! Fix it quick! I stop her before she gets out the door. "C'mon Wendy. I was joking. I didn't know that was your news. Do your parents know?"

"Mom does. She's already planning my leave of absence. When Dad finds out, there's going to be hell to pay."

"Here I thought I was finally going to get that pardon. Guess not."

Wendy brushes that aside. "No, it won't be you. He's not very happy at how things are being run these days in our world. There're too many loose cannons out there. There's talk of increased regulation on the community."

I consider asking her if she's going to keep it, but I don't really feel like getting slapped this evening and assume she does.

"Would you like me down on one knee?" I could do much worse than a girl who is filthy rich, pretty, and is one of the A List superheroes. Not too bad for a scrub from the bush leagues like me.

"No! God! No!" The speed of her response is disheartening.

"Gee thanks!"

She punches me in the shoulder. "That's not it. We're not in love. Most days we're barely in like. You get under my skin, Cal, damn near every day! I have to leave the room sometimes because of it. That wouldn't work in a marriage. I want to wake up next to a man I love. Besides, I still think that Aphrodite will come to her senses."

"Most would say that she already has. So I'm thinking Rufus if it's a boy and Geraldine if it's a girl. What do you think?"

"I think you should stick to making powered battle suits and leave the other decisions to people who have a clue about the magic of life."

"Yeah, I suppose you can't mix magic and science. It's never pretty is it?"

She manages a smile. It looks like a weight has been lifted from her shoulders. "Thanks for not throwing some kind of tantrum or being an asshole, Cal. I'm not sure how things will work when the baby is born, but if you want involvement, you'll have it. If you don't, I won't force you. I don't need an answer for a long time either, so think it over and get back to me when you're sure."

She leaves me with feelings of inadequacy. I'm not exactly good boyfriend material! What kind of father could I possibly make? It's not like I've got a helluva role model to draw on. Sorry Dad. I'm just calling it the way I see it.

Conflicting themes in my life, just like trying to mix science and magic. That's never a good idea. Then again, who knows?

• • •

"I know you worry about your new armor, but don't you think you should, I don't know get out of it every so often? It probably smells awful in there." Sheila comments. As I turn away, she makes the "cuckoo" motion with her index finger and points at me. Anemone laughs.

"I'm fine. Trust me on that. Never been better." Things are actually pretty good right now. I'm back to being the second most powerful person on this team and the couple of battles we'd been in since then helped me justify my decision to accept some, for lack of better words, outside assistance in making this new suit.

"If you say so," she replies. Further comments are interrupted by the monitor screen barking to life. Bolt Action's frame fills it.

"Stringel, Dozier! Where's La Guardia?"

"In her room."

"Get her, now!" He's barking like he's still in the Corps.

"Something going down?" She-Dozer asks.

"Yeah. It must be your birthday come early, Stringel."

"What?"

"Patterson's going down. Jade Lyoness just escaped from an attack by Ultraweapon. She found something really big and sent it to me."

"How big?"

"Life imprisonment kind of big. He's got a new robot prototype that runs off of a nuclear core. I'm not even certain how many treaties that violates, but I've already contacted the Olympians and the Oval Office and everyone is onboard. Are you interested?"

I whistle. Type D Warbots are the largest bots that can run off of current powercell technology and only for a limited duration. For some reason, putting a reactor in a robot and letting it wander around is universally frowned on by diplomats.

"Wouldn't miss it for the world." And here I thought this was going to be a slow day.

"Good. Get airborne and we'll coordinate things in the sky. I doubt he's going to just surrender and we expect heavy resistance."

• • •

Patterson is waiting for us. Promethia's main headquarters is an armored fortress. Some of his security force wants no part of this battle and flees, but others don't care or are programmed to do their master's bidding. As one of the "heavy hitters" my job is to clear out the bigger robots. I also have a "special mission" from Bolt Action - lure Patterson out and engage him.

I'm just the man for the job. Strafing the Type D Warbots on the perimeter, I vent my figurative spleen. "Can't you feel it, Ultrafailure? Your whole little empire is crumbling. You brought this on yourself, you know?"

Nothing yet. I guess I'll keep poking him in the eye with a stick until I get a reaction.

"Are you going to go out like a man with your self-destruct, or do I get to see you brought into court like the craven mongrel you are? Word of advice Lazarus - don't bother saying you're sorry to the judge. It never works."

"I will make sure you die, Stringel!"

"You're not man enough," I launch a steady stream of grenades into a Warbot until the shields drop and the explosions blow it to the ground. "Is it me or are your playthings getting easier to destroy? Where's your newest creation, Laz? Is it just as flawed as the rest of your stuff?"

"Just keep running your mouth, you little shit! You'll get yours."

Maybe I'm having too much fun, but I can't stop myself. "Listen, we all know you ran out of good ideas after synth-muscle. Never could come close after that, could you? Your engineers are the ones that did the real work. You just like to dress up and play superhero."

There he is. "About time you came out to play, Ultraflaw. Let's dance!"

My shielding is upgraded. My weaponry is better than ever and I have dozens of superheroes on my side. For once, I have the upper hand. On my back, I slide the powercell bazooka into position and knife through the sky right at him.

From the mini-gun, plasma darts cross the distance and spatter on his shielding. His force blasters knock me off course as our dance goes freestyle. We circle and I almost bracket him, micro seconds from firing my big stick, but Bolt Action comes from nowhere and smashes into Patterson knocking my target out of the weapon's firing arc.

I keep after him, but am limited to plasma, grenades, and force blasters. The effing heroes keep getting in the way. Apollo this time, spewing volcanic magma from his chariot. Zeus seconds later, blazing with electrical power. My life has been leading up to this, but even my finest moment is being thwarted by these damn heroes.

"Get out of my damn way!" I shout over the open channel. "Patterson is mine!"

They won't listen. They keep interfering. I can't get a lock. His shields are down to the point that this weapon has a better than fifty percent chance of killing him. I like those odds.

"Cal! I need your help," Wendy's voice reaches out to me. I ignore her.

"Stringel!" she won't be deterred. "Get your sorry ass over here now! We've got a major problem."

"I'm busy. Try again later."

"If you're not right next to me in thirty seconds I will beat the living shit out of you!"

Okay, she's pissed about something. I'd better find out what. Damn it to hell!

Breaking off, I look for her. Whatever she wants, it better be important! Oh, so that's Patterson's new toy. I'm not ashamed to say that I'm impressed by what the engineers here dreamed up.

It stands nearly fifty feet tall and has the X arms like the Type C and the hammer like head, but it's friggin' huge! The lasers are arrays, spinning like my mini-gun and spitting out an endless stream of red death. I find Wendy, at the base of a building.

"You've still got that launcher? Good. I'll try to knock it off balance. You hit it in the back or a knee and the others will try and finish it."

"But Patterson?"

"He's almost down. Let it go and quit being an idiot! That thing can kill us all."

She's right. I know she is. It doesn't make it any easier to swallow. Brave young woman. She goes flying off into danger while pregnant with my kid. That's right, Cal. Get your damn priorities straight! She sways it with the power of an F-4 and Bolt Action hits one of the knees unbalancing the robot. Ares hurls a tank at it as I dodge streams of energy and circle behind it. I line up my bazooka and look for something that might be important. Finding nothing, I line it up where it should do enough damage to knock it over and fire. *Weapon discharge. Brace for impact.*

The overloaded powercell hits it like a sledgehammer, releasing megajoules of stored energy and wrecking the entire hip assembly. The prototype topples to the ground. Heroes swarm it. I join in with my energy weapons.

My taunts come back to me with an ominous message of impending doom. "We've got to get the core out in case he tries to detonate it. Move! Move!"

I use my mini-gun like a surgeon's scalpel. Armor and the internal structure fall to the side. There! Surrounded by heat exchangers and shining like a small star. It's not as big as I thought it would be. This isn't a case of Blue Wire/Red Wire. This is a case of rip the damn thing out before he kills us all.

Pull! I yank the assembly free and toss it aside. A minute or two later, they drag Patterson in his battered suit over.

"Bravo, Stringel. You're right, I could have detonated it and killed us all. You've saved me the trouble."

"What the hell are you talking about?"

"Tell me one thing, idiot, what do you think is going to happen now that it is no longer tied to any heat exchangers?"

Shit! He's right. I whip my head around and engage thermals. The thing is white hot. "We need to get it out of here or Los Angeles is a goner!" I look for a savior. Bolt Action can't stand after being pulled out from under the prototype. None of the other flyers have the strength except for Wendy using cyclones. She's already trying to use her wind powers to air cool the core. It's only delaying the inevitable.

I meet her gaze and she steps forward, just like a real hero would. I stop her.

"No. My mess. I'll fly it out into the Pacific and go underwater. You have to push back the jet stream and keep anything from coming ashore."

"Cal! I'm not that strong."

"Whatever," I brush aside her complaint, "Just do it, Wendy!"

I drop the mini-gun and shed whatever weight I can. Grabbing the core, I take off heading west. By the time I see the ocean, my shields are buckling and God only knows how much radiation is around. It's interfering with the instruments, but my suit can make it. The temp in the suit is rising and the core I'm holding is already spot welded to my arms. We're going to have to go into the water together. The core will split open and then ... it's boom-boom time.

My suit can't survive the beating much longer. This is the end and I know it. Hopefully there's enough time for some final loose ends. I cut off the garbled receiver and the noise of people trying to say things to me.

Cutting on the transmitter, I know what I need to do.

"Alright everyone, this is the end of the line for Mechani-Cal, but I'm not going quietly. I'm releasing my memoirs right this second. They're being updated with my final words. Dad, you tried. Thanks I guess. Mom, maybe this will finally get you back in good standing with your friends. Wendy, thanks for everything. I mean it. I always liked Gabrielle for a girl and James for a boy, serious this time. All the proceeds from sales of my book are to go into a trust for that kid. I can't really say I'm in my right mind because I'm holding a god damn fusion reactor core in my hands! Read my words people and hold the powers that be accountable. They might be super powerful, but they aren't super human! Remember that. Stacy, sorry we couldn't make it work. Patterson … if they have any stones, they'll fry you. Overlord, this squares us in my books, sorry if I just let the world know you're still out there. My bad. Tough shit. What else? What else? Hey, do I finally get that pardon? I've been working my ass …"

Transmission Ends

Epilogue the First
A San Francisco Fiasco

The cool breeze off the bay keeps blowing my hair across my face as we look down through the clear bottom of Apollo's chariot at the convoy leaving the federal courthouse in San Francisco. Despite long months of legal maneuvering and testimony, Lazarus is going to the SuperMax in North Dakota for a life sentence with no chance of parole and legal experts were saying that the Supreme Court were unlikely to even hear any appeal his high-priced legal team could come up with. When the sentence was read, Lazarus didn't have a meltdown like I expected.

As they led him away in chains, he mouthed the words, "You will regret this."

The Olympians and many of the Guardians are here to make sure there are no problems and help improve our image which has taken a beating in the public eye as of late.

"You're pretty quiet, Stacy. I'm just glad it's finally over. Aren't you?" Holly says to me.

"Yeah," I say feeling tired. There is no sensation of a weight being lifted off my shoulders – no feeling of closure.

"I thought he was going to get away with a shorter sentence when they started trying to pin the blame for the detonation on Stringel."

If Holly is trying to get me to open up, bringing up Cal won't help things. I am still conflicted about his death and with the release of his "tell all," things hadn't really gotten much better. Cal acquired something of a cult hero status because of his book and I'm told that it doesn't paint a very favorable image of me or most of the heroes in general.

Truthfully, I still hadn't mustered up the courage to read more than a couple of pages. Family, friends, and even casual acquaintances that had were more than willing to chime in with their two cents. The ones who hated him, most notably Holly, were quick to point out that the beginning of our relationship had all the classic indicators of Stockholm syndrome.

At the same time others, like the Bugler and the rest of the Gulf Coast Guardians painted Cal in a kinder light.

• • •

Still on crutches the Bugler had approached me after the empty casket funeral and said, "Miss? I just wanted to say that I'm sorry."

I responded, "I am too. I'm just sorry that I never got my memories back."

What I didn't tell him was that I'd been erecting my own mental blocks and walling those memories off. Part of me said I was better off not remembering all the details of my relationship with Cal. The less charitable part of me said I was being a coward and running away from something that might end up causing me pain.

The Bugler smiled, "If you ever do get them back and need a person to talk to, feel free to call. I met him when he was just a petty criminal taking out his frustrations on the rest of the world, but when the world needed him the most, he turned himself around. I know he'd just make some kind of crass comment along the lines that all he was looking for was a paycheck and a pardon, but I'm pretty sure the real reason was you."

"Thank you, but I think you're giving me too much credit," I said, looking for a way to graciously exit this conversation before it got more awkward than it was already.

"You're welcome," he replied with his southern drawl. "No. I usually don't tangle with the uber villain types, just the everyday sort. But that helps me know how they think. Before you, he didn't really care about anything or anyone. You gave him a reason to start caring and it stuck with him even after the two of you broke up. That's what really loving someone can do for you and as my wife would say, that's more powerful than any sonic bugle or superpower out there."

I managed to stammer a few more things to him before begging off. His comments had cracked the emotional shell I'd carefully maintained concerning the late Calvin Stringel.

Ever since I'd gotten my powers, people would say how guys would do "anything" to be with me and Cal seemingly did. Wendy and I were never really close and never talked much. Despite the press and most everyone else wanting to ask her about Cal and the revelations from the book, she rarely ever spoke about him except in general terms. That said, in a moment of candidness about a week after the explosion off the coast of Los Angeles, I ran into her in the Senate waiting room where we were called to testify before her father's committee. She said that she thought, half the reason Cal killed Mather was for what he'd done to the two of them and the other half was that he didn't think I'd ever take him back because of it.

• • •

"Earth to Stacy, are you still there?" Holly asks, bringing me back to the present.

"Yes," I answer. "I was just thinking that I need a vacation."

"You've definitely earned one. Where are you thinking about going?"

"Somewhere quiet to get away from everything for a week. Maybe a small tropical island, I don't know. It's been a rough year."

Holly nods as we adjust our path for the turn the convoy below us is taking. "Sounds like a plan. If you want company, let me know. If you want to go solo, that's okay too."

I start to reply, but a loud rumbling catches my attention. The source is a half-built office building and it's collapsing. My mental funk clears and I start acting. A quick scan of the area with my powers shows the building is thankfully vacant. The main risk is damage to the surrounding buildings that aren't and to the convoy we're escorting.

"I don't sense anyone inside," I say over Holly telling Kevin to get the chariot closer so Robin can use her force shields to stop the flying debris. When it comes down to it, we're professional heroes and being together for over a decade has made us the best at what we do.

The only problem with this is the nagging feeling that this isn't a coincidence.

WhirlWendy, flying nearby, helps Hera with the dust and debris. Between the two, the cloud dissipates rapidly. The things that become readily apparent are that it was only the front of the building that collapsed with the other three walls still intact. Also, there is very little in the way of debris. Finally, there's the matter of all the robots pouring out of the three-sided trap. There are hundreds of them, mostly the ball type robots, but there are some larger Warbots in the mix as well.

"Ambush!" Robin shouts as the laser blast emerge from the shadow of the trap. She protects us, but the staggering amount of power is like buckshot to the buildings behind us that are full of onlookers.

I glance at the convoy and see it stopped. It looks like some kind of cylinder with a manhole cover disguise on top has bisected the armored van carrying Lazarus. He's probably already out of his shackles and changing into an Ultraweapon suit.

Holly sees it too and throws one of her energy spears at the van, hoping to put a stop to things before it gets any messier. It splashes ineffectively on a shield coming from the pillar. Realization dawns on me. If this was just going to be a jailbreak, he wouldn't have brought so many robots. Lazarus wants a war in the middle of downtown San Francisco and doesn't care about the collateral damage!

Robin and Athena bark orders. When the chariot is within thirty feet of the ground, I leap off and brace my body for the landing, regretting that I didn't wear my powered armor that Cal made for me. My mental blasts are more effective against living opponents, but they can still do the job against the smaller robots.

I join the woefully outgunned federal agents and SWAT officers on the ground scattering from the vehicles, some already burning. Concentrating, I focus my energy into a tight stream and unleash it on the first group of balls I see. There are so many of them that it's nearly impossible to miss and the area is so dense with buildings that heroes like Wendy and Bolt Action can't unleash the full force of their powers.

We're in trouble!

A pulse cannon love tap sends me back into a mailbox. I finish ripping the hunk of twisted metal out of the ground and hurl it back at the approaching wall of bots. Gouts of fire slag at least twenty of them as Apollo summons jets of magma. Ares is smashing away with his titanium mace but the robots around him suddenly detonate sending him flying through the air.

"Cover me, Aphrodite!" Zeus shouts, crouching low and trying to make himself as small a target as possible. He's charging up for a full release of his lightning powers and needs me to buy him time. Ripping a parking meter out of the concrete and using the ball of metal and stone at the end as my own club, I jump in front of him and go back to my old high school field hockey days on the closest group of robots. My brute strength helps clear the ones in the immediate area and my mind blasts take out some in the second wave.

"I can handle these, Zeus. Try and take out one of the big ones."

"Right," he answers with a grunt. "Here it goes!"

Energy erupts from his body like a horizontal geyser, ripping a jagged line through the opposing robots. The discharge makes many of the ones in the path explode and that causes an even wider swath of destructions. The mass of energy slams into the leg of one of the large Warbots and sends it crashing to the ground.

Hermes zips up the path Zeus just cleared to get to the back of the pack and start attacking them from there. The danger is everywhere, but we're starting to take the momentum.

"Energy building up!" Zeus says pointing at the shielded cylinder protecting Lazarus.

We dive to the ground as it pulses outward, killing the few remaining agents nearby and even destroying some of the robots. Sadly, that probably bothers Lazarus more. He's so far beyond gone now.

There's a lull in the action as the remaining robots hold their fire. They're waiting for his command. I search the sky looking for the shape so many used to look up to and find it, floating above the wreckage. His color scheme is different – red on black.

"When you finish playing with these toys," he announces, "Come down to the waterfront and that's where the real fun begins."

Bolt Action launches himself, but Ultraweapon turns him aside with a computer assisted burst from his force blasters and starts to fly away. I hit him with my mind blast, but it only manages to shove his suit as his shields absorb it along with a spear from Athena. Zeus can't fire until he finishes recharging and Ultraweapon is already out of range as his remaining robots resume fire and give us something else to worry about.

Leaping next to me, Holly hurls another spear and says, "He's got us dancing to his tune. If this is his version of a distraction, I hate to think of what's waiting for us."

"He forgot one thing," I shout and blast another robot to pieces with my mind. Lazarus has gone too far this time and needs to be stopped.

"What's that?"

"He used to lead, but I was always the better dancer!"

• • •

We're tired and more than a little banged up as we advance to the waterfront. Keisha sprints back from her scouting sortie and blurts out what's ahead.

"He's got ten more Warbots and another one of those Behemoth things from Los Angeles!"

Of course, it all makes sense. Why would he just build one atomic powered robot?

Hera puts down the communicator she was using and scowls, saying, "The Navy has a carrier off the coast. They've got a squadron launching, with an ETA of thirty minutes. They need us to keep them close to the shore and not let them further into the city."

Athena nods, "We can assume that Ultraweapon already intercepted this message and knows what's coming."

Flying over the virtual river of people running for their lives below us, we race headlong into battle.

• • •

Fifteen minutes have passed, though it feels like hours. I'd check, but I can barely move. Ares might be seriously hurt. He'd taken out a Warbot and was emerging from the wreckage when Lazarus hit Frankie point blank in the back with everything he had. When Ares landed, the Behemoth stepped on him.

The fight rages on, but my part in it is done. Lazarus turned on me next and neither of us held back. If I had my armor, I might have won. Instead, he's holding me up by my neck, choking me while I fire ever weakening mental bolts at him. I'm spent and he's toying with me. Even with my superhuman endurance, I'll pass out any second now. Part of me wonders if he'll just keep squeezing until I'm dead and if my powers will transfer to either my brother or sister when I die like they did with the original Hephaestus. A male Aphrodite? Now there's a stupid thought.

"I think this is a good look for you, Aphrodite. This is really your own fault. If you hadn't been such a whore, none of this would have happened!"

I try to say, "Go to hell," but don't have any air to do it.

"No matter what else happens today, I'll go down in history as the man that destroyed The Olympians!"

His statement is punctuated by a large explosion. One of his six remaining Warbots just went down in a big way. His grip loosens and I suck in the most awful smelling lungful of air ever, but it tastes like life itself to me. Even with my blurry vision, I can see two shapes approaching from the wreckage of the large robot. Lazarus tosses me aside and leaps into the air to attack them. The first one is dressed in some kind of a solid red outfit and the other one is in a suit of armor. I don't recognize either of them.

Ultraweapon's opening volley strikes an expanding field of power surrounding the red hero. It grows into a huge figure, lifting Red into the air and into the center of the humanoid energy construct. Who in the hell is that? The "arm" of the energy being swats Lazarus aside as he pounces on the back of a Warbot, and rips an arm off of the big robot.

As impressive as that is, the armored hero is carrying what looks like a big pistol and fires it at the relatively pristine Behemoth. I can't tell if it's a slug, a missile, or a bolt of energy, but it rips through the shielding and wrecks one of the laser assemblies. Bolt Action had hit that thing twice already and did far less damage.

Who the hell are these guys?

Lazarus turns on the other armored suit and they both go skyward and try to beat the tar out of each other. It looks like Ultraweapon is faster, but the new guy is better armed, if that's possible. The pace picks up and they're moving too fast for my tired eyes to follow.

Staggering to my feet, I know I should pitch in and help the others. The Red hero with the giant energy form is wrestling with two of the Warbots while Wendy, Bolt Action, Zeus, and Apollo are working as a team against two more. Concentrating, I fire off a streamer of mental energy that smacks into the back of the one Wendy managed to knock on its side into the larger Behemoth. The shielding of the two robots is nullified by their contact and the two are momentarily vulnerable. The elongated head of the Behemoth takes another shot from that hand canon the unidentified armored hero just shot.

Did he beat Lazarus that easily? No, there's Ultraweapon coming back for round two.

I try a telepathic message to the new guy, partly to warn him and partly to see if I can get a glimpse of who these new heroes are.

Nothing! Too much shielding. As far as I can tell, nobody is inside that suit. Maybe it's a robot and I can't get anything off of it.

Diving out of the way as the Red hero leaps by me and into the Behemoth, I forget about trying to figure out identities and focus on what I'm supposed to be doing.

Red's energy form is only about a third of the size of Patterson's monster. It's like watching a midget attack a full grown person, but Red is one very determined midget. I add what little I have to offer as his presence drives the giant robot backward in the direction of the water. The sound of metal ripping fills the air as Red tears at the damage created by his teammate's earlier shot. Something begins to form behind the Behemoth. It's Wendy, she's pulling up a waterspout out of the bay. Red keeps it busy while the Gulf Coast Guardian drops tons of water on them both. The electrical energy released is enough to knock Red off, but he picks up an abandoned city bus and hurls it into the failing robot's upper torso. Aided by Wendy's wind gusts, it causes the thing to fall into the water.

Red wastes no time and leaps onto the fallen mass of metal. He's going to rip out the core as Wendy continues to rain down water to prevent the core from overheating. I get the strangest feeling that Wendy has worked with Red and the new suit before.

There's still the danger that Lazarus could detonate the thing, so I spin and look. No, the new hero is all over him spewing energy and weapon fire. The Ultraweapon suit is in complete defensive mode. Another powerful blast knocks my ex from the sky and he plows into the ground.

The suit's shields must be down, I can sense his panic. If I can get a line of sight on him, I can stun him and end this. Digging deep, I scrounge for whatever strength I have left and awkwardly sprint in the direction of his disjointed thoughts.

When I crest the pile of rubble, the other armored hero has Ultraweapon held up with both arms. A fresh ripple of raw panic emanates from Lazarus along with recognition. He knows who the suit really is! I send enough energy to stun him, but before it strikes the two are cocooned in a massive high voltage discharge. By the time my bolt hits, Lazarus is already dead.

The new suit, I can't call him or it a hero if he just executes a person like that, lets loose a second discharge. That's just overkill. I wait to see if it does a third, but it just drops the fried Ultraweapon armor like so much rubbish.

"You didn't have to do that!" I scream at the armor. It turns and faces me. There's barely a scratch on the damn thing! Lazarus never stood a chance.

"Who are you? What are you?"

It says nothing, but flies into the sky and attacks the last remaining Warbot and I'm left staring at the twisted shell of metal and flesh that used to tell me how much he cared. Bile creeps up into the back of my throat as tears roll down my cheeks. The new armored fighter knew Lazarus and hated him enough to electrocute him and then do it again just to be certain.

There are only two people I know that despise Ultraweapon that much and could do it wearing a suit of armor. If the Overlord had a suit like that he wouldn't stop with just killing Lazarus. He'd be killing us now, but he's not. Instead, he's exchanging a fist bump with his partner and ignoring the shouts of everyone else. They're leaving. Artificial intelligences don't "hate" and they don't fist bump. That's got to be a real person!

The only other candidate … *No! It can't be. He's dead. Isn't he?*

I move away from the stench around the corpse and walk down to the waterline. Standing there, I ponder the ramifications until an equally exhausted Holly finds me. "Stacy, are you okay?"

"I'm banged up, but I'll live. How's Frankie?"

She answers, "Not good. The Chariot's taking him to the nearest hospital along with a couple of others. Robin wants me to try and figure out who that duo was."

"Did you ask Wendy? I think she might have an idea." I might as well, but I want to be sure.

"She left right after the new guys."

It does seem like she has something to hide. "Lazarus said he wanted to go down as the man who destroyed us. He almost did it."

"Well, he didn't. We're going to be shorthanded for awhile, but we'll get by. It probably means you won't be able to take vacation anytime soon."

Inside my mind, I'm already dismantling the barriers I'd made around my lost memories. I have to know the truth!

"S'okay, Holly. Maybe I'll just curl up with a book instead."

Epilogue the Second
The Inverted Hot Fudge Sundae

Landing the hoversled and fighting off the butterflies circling in my stomach, I take a deep breath and look at my destination. All the countless dangers I've faced and I'm scared at what I might find under this beat up old grain silo.

"Get a grip, Stacy," I say trying to will my nervousness away. "If he's here, he's still alive."

But what do I do then? It took all this time to finally remember everything about Cal and why I was so taken with him. If I'm being honest with myself, I stopped trying after his death in Los Angeles, but after the fiasco in San Francisco, I slowly reassembled my memories of this shithole. Two days ago, I remembered everything.

Climbing off the vehicle, I walk in the direction of a crumbling barn next to that silo, retracing the steps that I only now remember. I feel giddy like a schoolgirl and struggle against getting my hopes up. A hint of fear crosses my heart. What if he doesn't want me anymore? Without the memories of why I found him great, I wasn't very kind to him. For everything that's been said about him, he can hold a monstrous grudge.

Holly would mock me and tell me that I could do a million times better than Cal Stringel, but she's wrong. He's a great guy and I finally remember why he's so special. At best, he tolerated the glitz and glamour of my world, but he'd bend over backward to share his world with me. Unlike Lazarus, he had a streak of humility and could stomach being defeated without it occupying his every waking moment or me being more successful than him. He could handle that and even took pride in being the "second most powerful" member of his team behind Wendy. Much like my namesake goddess had fallen for her inventor, I did as well. Cal has a genius that reaches beyond just his suit and I thought I could bring out the best in him.

Thanks to Lazarus, I reverted to my typical bitchy self and didn't give Cal that, but he found a way to succeed on his own. Maybe that was for the best. I don't know. I'm babbling in my own mind and literally can't wait to see that armor he built. How'd he do it? I've learned quite a bit about armor and armor design, but that set that killed Ultraweapon shouldn't exist. No way! There's not enough space on the chassis for all the things he was doing with it.

In the barn, five Type B robots come to life. Their weapons are trained on me. I recognize a Mindwiper on one of them and know that the occupants take their privacy seriously. I calm my nerves and say, "I'm here to see Cal. It's me, Stacy."

My heart thumps when they move aside and I reach the access panel. *8675309*

The code still works! The door slides open and I step into it. After a few seconds, the door closes. Muzak starts up as the lift descends. *Cute Cal. Very cute.* An instrumental version of *Just a Friend.* How appropriate.

At the bottom of the shaft, I compose myself as the door opens. This is it. Whatever happens next, I'll know that the moment I remembered everything, I came running and I hope it's enough.

There are two guys sitting in front of the main console playing a shooter game. Neither of them is Cal. They pause the game.

"Hi, I'm Stacy is Cal here?"

The large, thick one must be Hillbilly Bobby. Cal once said this was his hideout before Bobby disappeared. I don't know the other one, but odds are that he's Red.

"He's back there ma'am," Red answers, sounding kind of goofy in an "aw shucks" way. I get a grin on my face, but there's a little voice in the back of my head still wondering how he survived a nuclear explosion.

The door opens and I step into what used to be his bedroom. It's more of a workshop now. It looks like there's been a bunch of remodeling. "Hi!" I force as much good spirits into my greeting. He's standing, unharmed, and in good shape. It is more than I could hope for. Behind him is that massive suit that everyone is still talking about.

"Nice to see you again," he says in guarded tones. "How long have you known?"

"I didn't for sure. I was just rolling the dice. When my memories came back I finished your book and realized you gave the wrong location for this shit … place." I'm on unsteady footing here. Before, he wouldn't mind me calling his base names.

"What can I do for you?"

"You can start by coming over here and giving me a hug. I never thought I'd see you again!"

He complies, but hesitates when I kiss him. I start to wonder if things are screwed thing up beyond repair.

"You're not that surprised to see me, Aphrodite?"

"When you're in the business as long as I've been, you can never be sure unless you see the body with your own eyes. Please, call me Stacy."

"Okay, Stacy." Cal says it so slowly that it doesn't sound right. He's almost as nervous as I am. I can feel it rolling all over him. I feel his hurt and know that I was part of the cause. *Think, Stacy! Think! Break the ice.*

"So, why don't you tell me about that fancy suit of armor?"

"I'm not sure it would be a good idea."

"Please Cal, don't push me away. I just want a chance." If the real Aphrodite saw me right now, would she strip my powers for sounding so desperate? I'd like to think she'd be proud of me.

My eyes drift over to the workbench and I see a couple of pictures. One is WhirlWendy and the other is a tiny baby.

I was so fixated on the armor and Cal that I didn't even notice the playpen in the corner with all the toys next to a full drum kit. "Oh lord. I didn't know you and Wendy had gotten together. I'm sorry. I don't want to …"

Shit! He's already moved on.

Cal laughs. "No, we're not together. She brings Gabby around on weekends and when she needs a sitter. It is nice having a place that no one knows about to keep our daughter safe from anyone who would try to use her to harm us."

I want to smile, knowing that he's available and I still have a chance. "Don't worry, Cal. I won't tell anyone where this place really is. So what are your plans? Athena and Hera want these new heroes found and recruited. They were even talking about opening slots on the Olympians."

This time Cal really laughs. "It would almost be worth it to see the look on Crenshaw's face. No, I'm not sure I was meant to be a hero. I wasn't very good at it."

"You're not going back to the other side, are you?" I saw that suit in action and don't want to end up fighting it.

"Definitely no. I was a lousy villain," he says, shaking his head.

"Cal? I'm a little lost. Where are you going with this?"

"Meh, the only time I'm worth a shit is when the world needs saving. You and damn near everyone else said as much at the funeral. Hard to believe I finally got my pardon, isn't it? Anyway, don't call me and Larry for a bank robbery; call us when it really means something."

"Larry?" It takes a second for me to put it together. "That guy on the couch is Imaginary Larry?"

"Not anymore. I call him Extraordinary Larry. He's wearing the Grey Logger's old necklace and is only about half as strong as he was when he was living his multiple personality life. The power was too much for his mind and it overwhelmed him. The necklace dampens it down to where he can finally think straight. Still, even at half his potential, he kicks some serious ass! Admittedly, a technohermit like me probably isn't the best guy to help him reintegrate into society, but we've been making steady progress. Last time Wendy was here, she took Larry into Mobile and helped him shop."

"She's semi-retired from the Guardians. Is that because, she's on this team as well?"

"Yeah, she's the third member of the Reinforcements."

"Reinforcements? Sounds catchy." Larry, Wendy, and Cal's new suit make a formidable team.

"Yeah. Call us when you need us, but make sure it's damn important. Don't waste our time on the everyday garbage."

"Back to the armor…" I say.

"You're not going to let it go are you?"

"I'm dying here, Cal. I may not be in your league when it comes to tinkering, but that thing can't possibly work the way it does! Spill!"

"I cheated," he says like it explains everything.

"Cheated? You can't cheat? There's only so much room in that armor - in that hand cannon - it … they can't do what they were doing. How can you cheat?"

"Remember that thing with Tyrannosorcerer Rex?"

"That lizard guy who wanted to take over the world? I read the report, but it wasn't that complete. Didn't he turn your armor and Andydroid to stone? Explain it to me."

"He had these portal things. The translation is close to Mirrors of Movement. I shoved a small GPS through one of the shards and found his main base about thirty miles away. He had a few more of these mirror things there too."

Cal carefully picks up two identical shaped crystals and places them on the bench next to each other. He runs a wire into one and it pops out the other one. "This is how I cheat. There is no ammunition in that suit. I only have enough powercells installed to make it walk for about ten minutes. What is in the suit are dozens of portals inside protective casings running the power from this base into the armor. The prison cells downstairs have been converted into ammo magazines and my main weaponry. C'mon, I'll show you."

He's on a roll. I've got him talking about his armor. I couldn't stop him if I strip and say, "Take Me." Well, maybe I could, but I'll hold onto that thought for later.

I follow him down to where he held me prisoner for those awful two weeks. A voice interrupts my journey. "It's nice to see you again, Aphrodite."

Spinning, I see Andydroid's face. It's attached to an old Type A robot body, but it is him. "Andydroid! It's good to see you."

"It is good to be seen," the robot says. "Although you have encountered the replacement my creator manufactured using an old backup of my knowledgebase. Perhaps one day I will meet my new brother."

"How did you get turned back?"

"After translating a number of books, Cal was able to reverse the magic that petrified me on this portion on my body and is supposed to be getting me a new body. It should be noted that he is behind schedule, again."

My head spins. Cal? Reversing magic?

"I'm working on it, Type Andy. We'll get you set up right. I'm still holding out hope that we can get one of those Type E Behemoth frames. With the portals, we could power that thing up right and arm you to the teeth!" Cal exclaims.

"Magic?" I ask.

"It's a new hobby. I'm studying sixty-five million year old serpent sorcery. Before I gave Larry the necklace, I was using it because the magic in it lets me translate whatever I hear or read. When I cleaned out Rex's hidden base, I found all these spell books written in serpent runes. Imagine my surprise when I found out my translation skills worked on them too. Here watch this."

He concentrates and a bottle of water floats off the counter and into my hands. He looks visibly shaken by the effort. "That's impressive."

"Yeah, I'm a long ways from using it for real and most of the spells won't work because I'm warm blooded, but I picked up a couple of things along the way. After a few months, I didn't need the necklace anymore, so I went and got Larry. He's such a newbie, but I'm training him up right."

Cal is so casual about everything. I roll my eyes at the thought of him mentoring someone with Larry's level of power and say, "I can only imagine. So you just decided to start learning lizard magic on a whim? That's pretty crazy, even for you, Cal. Okay, what exactly is this?"

The gun emplacement takes up most of the space that used to be the cell block. It looks like it should be mounted on a tank or something.

"This is my railgun. It's only ten megajoules. The navy has a bigger one, but that's enough to get my slugs moving so fast they'll rip through shielding and armor like butter. It's my biggest stick, but not my only stick."

"You built ... a railgun?"

He nods and says, "Just a small one. Andy helped after I freed him. With the portal magic, it fires here in the base, but the shell comes out of the tip of my handheld which is really the end of the barrel. Neat huh? Next to it is my fifty caliber shells, my pulse cannons, and my forty mike mikes. Patterson wasn't fighting me; he was fighting my whole base. He didn't stand a chance."

"This is nothing short of amazing, Cal. You combined magic and science to make a suit of armor."

"Thanks," he says sheepishly and points to a chair. "I don't even need to be in the suit. I usually run the armor remotely from here. Were you trying to probe me at the battle?"

Nodding, I say, "Yes, but I thought it was blocked by the shielding."

"Probably. But even if you'd gotten by it, I was here ... a few thousand miles away. I've been here since building the suit that was nuked in Los Angeles."

"Really? The whole time?"

"Yeah, the Gulf Coasters kept wondering why I never got out of my new suit. They thought I'd gone off the deep end."

"Wow," that's about all I can come up with.

"Yeah. Anyway, I was here the whole time, hanging out with Bobby, after I figured out I could use the pieces of Lizard Boy's broken portal. Everything was running through all those shards. Hell, Patterson was trying to kill me! I wasn't just going to stand there and let him do it. It amazes me that people think I'm that stupid."

Finally, an explanation that made some sense! "What did you say to him before you killed him? I was only close enough to sense his fear."

"I told him that I delivered on my promise. He never saw me coming for him until it was too late." Cal stops and looks pensive before continuing, "You're not here to give me a hard time about whacking his worthless ass are you?"

"No," I say. "Lazarus made his own bed."

"Thanks, Stacy. The last thing I wanted to do today was get into an argument. Anyway, I'd have never been able to build a suit that could match up to his with all his money and engineers, so I had to go outside of the box and mix magic into it. I still need a name though. The press keeps calling it Firepower and Arsenal, but I'm thinking old school."

He gets that grin on his face like a cat ready to pounce. "What?" I ask.

"Well, I hear the name Ultraweapon is vacant. I beat the guy and I think that entitles me to a few things. That makes me the reigning champ until someone can take that name away from me and the Megasuit!"

"He's probably rolling in his grave right now. It's brilliant! You're brilliant." I grab him.

"Ow! Easy there goddess. You've got a firm grip." He pauses and then continues, "Where does this leave us?"

We're so close. It only takes a quick stretch for me to kiss him. This time he returns it with more eagerness. "I'm me again. I'm not that bitchy type A superheroine who isn't sure what she wants. Plus, there's a nasty rumor about me that I fall hard for guys with hot suits of armor and there's nothing on the planet that can touch yours. Maybe I can even convince you to upgrade mine."

I can sense his excitement overcoming his anxiety. "Oh, an armor groupie," he teases. "I'm not sure this is going to work and as far as an upgrade goes, can you afford my rate?"

We kiss until it is a struggle to control our emotions. This is what's been missing, the feelings he creates with all the strange ideas, utter nonsense, and flashes of brilliance that come from nowhere. "I can be quite persuasive and I brought a down payment. Can we go somewhere and negotiate? It might take awhile."

"I think we can do that," he says already panting a little. I might have been hugging him a bit too tightly.

"Good, I can't wait to get started. I've missed you, Cal."

"I've missed you more, Stacy. Thanks for coming back for me."

His heartfelt words give me pause. "Thanks for waiting. We've got some lost time to make up for. What do you want to do first?"

"Can I play Biz?" He asks and then winks. Thank God he's not serious!

"How about something other than that," I answer and then whisper my naughty little counter offer into his ear.

"Okay," he agrees. "For that he'd understand. I've got the ice cream and the chocolate syrup, but I don't have a localized gravity inhibitor."

I give him a mischievous smile and say, "But I bet you've got a bootleg set of plans in your database. C'mon, we can build one together and then I'll show you why I'm the love goddess."

About the Author

Jim Bernheimer is the author of two other novels and a short story collection. He lives in Chesapeake, Virginia with his wife and two daughters while trying desperately to write down all the strange ideas in his mind.

Other Books by the Author

Horror, Humor, and Heroes Volume I

Horror, Humor, and Heroes Volume II

Dead Eye: Pennies for the Ferryman

Spirals of Destiny Book One: Rider

Dead Eye 2: The Skinwalker Conspiracies (Coming Summer 2011)

Spirals of Destiny Book Two: Sorceress (Coming Winter 2011)

Made in the USA
San Bernardino, CA
30 May 2013